EBURY PRESS
BANARAS TALKIES

Satya Vyas is an award-winning author of five bestselling books, including *Banaras Talkies*, *Dilli Durbar* and *Chaurasi*. Born and brought up in Bokaro in Jharkhand, he has established his identity in audio and screen writing, as well as opened a new path in Hindi writing. The web series *Grahan* is based on his book *Chaurasi*. Along with writing, he also takes creative writing classes through various learning apps.

Himadri Agarwal is an editor, a translator and reader. She currently works at Yoda Press and will soon be starting an English PhD at the University of Maryland, College Park. When not buried in a book or busy with work, she enjoys playing *Dungeons & Dragons*, eating junk food or doing both things at the same time.

T0015710

Banaras Talkies

Satya Vyas

Translated by
Himadri Agarwal

EBURY
PRESS

An imprint of Penguin Random House

EBURY PRESS

USA | Canada | UK | Ireland | Australia
New Zealand | India | South Africa | China

Ebury Press is part of the Penguin Random House group of companies
whose addresses can be found at global.penguinrandomhouse.com

Published by Penguin Random House India Pvt. Ltd
4th Floor, Capital Tower 1, MG Road,
Gurugram 122 002, Haryana, India

Penguin
Random House
India

First published in Ebury Press by Penguin Random House India 2022

Copyright © Satya Vyas 2022
Translation copyright © Himadri Agarwal 2022

All rights reserved

10 9 8 7 6 5 4 3 2

This is a work of fiction. Names, characters, places and incidents are either the
product of the author's imagination or are used fictitiously, and any resemblance
to any actual person, living or dead, events or locales is entirely coincidental.

ISBN 9780143454595

Typeset in Adobe Caslon Pro by Manipal Technologies Limited, Manipal
Printed at Thomson Press India Ltd, New Delhi

This book is sold subject to the condition that it shall not, by way of trade
or otherwise, be lent, resold, hired out, or otherwise circulated without the
publisher's prior consent in any form of binding or cover other than that in
which it is published and without a similar condition including this condition
being imposed on the subsequent purchaser.

www.penguin.co.in

This book is a result of the translation initiatives of the Ashoka Centre for Translation

Hum Hain Kamaal Ke: How Wonderful We Are

This is Bhagwandas, Bau Sahib. Bhagwandas Hostel. When the curse of time and the force of English shortened Banaras Hindu University to BHU, then Bhagwandas Hostel, too, became B.D. Hostel. Time may have shortened its name, but it wasn't able to bring down its fame. Two hundred and forty B.D. Jeevis live in its 120 rooms even today.

What? What does this B.D. Jeevi mean?

That is why I say, Bau Sahib, that you should keep your eyes open. You see that banyan tree in front of the hostel? Read the graffiti there. It says: *Kripya buddhi jeevi kehkar apmaan na kare. Yahan B.D. Jeevi rehte hain.* Please do not insult us by calling us intellectuals. B.D. Jeevis live here.

Now you're probably wondering what a B.D. Jeevi is. Go to room number 73 and ask who Bhagwan Das was. Someone will reply, '*Ghanta!*' This is Jaivardhanji. Lecture, ghanta. Lecturer, ghanta. Bhagwan, ghanta. Bhagwandas, ghanta. Even though everything is as nonsensical to him as his metaphorical ghanta, he manages to score well enough to get under the skin of both professors and nerds. Those who say the earth is balanced on Shiva's trident are wrong. It is actually balanced on Jaivardhan's ghanta, and he himself is balanced on his favourite idiom. He can start and end every discussion with a single idiom.

If you move further ahead, you will see the smoke from room 79. Arre bhai, don't worry! There is no fire. The only foreigner in Bhagwandas, Anurag De, must be smoking. He is a 'foreigner' because his ancestors were Bangladeshi, but the last two generations have been professionals in Mughalsarai. Come on! Professional means professional lawyers, Bau Sahib! Don't go down the wrong lane. Anyway, also keep in mind that because he is a Bengali, he is "Dada" to all of Bhagwandas. Even "Dada Bhaiya" to a few juniors. He speaks in cricket metaphors; he is the— what is the word—he is the encyclopaedia of cricket.

If this professor taught as smoothly as Sachin, then it would be worth it.

Arre! Is this idiot giving a lecture or is it Garner delivering a bouncer? Going right over my head!

Did you see that girl? She could have hit a perfect glance, I tell you!

He could have delivered a lecture on the difference between pinch-hitting and hard-hitting. He is, in fact, the one to have conferred Mark Greatbatch's title 'Father of Pinch-Hitting' on him. Dada is the only one in the country who understands the Da Vinci Code to unravel the Duckworth Lewis method. It was the semi-final of the 1987 World Cup. Sunil Gavaskar had been bowled out by Phillip DeFreitas in his second over itself, and six-year-old Anurag De began to holler, 'Fix hai! Fix hai!' His father thought he was saying, 'Six hai! Six hai!' If only his father had understood him that day! The man's carelessness is the reason why a crime like match-fixing has become so widespread.

Okay, okay, you're not interested in cricket. But you *are* interested in the girls' hostel, right? Then, in room number 79 itself, meet Dada's roommate Suraj. Even his father's name doesn't indicate that he's Brahmin. I don't know about other places, but Bhagwandas at least has no dearth of informants. Details of seven generations of his family were immediately dug out and he became the Baba of the college. Suraj to the faculty, Baba to friends. Baba is particularly interested in women. He has every update on the BHU girls' hostel, and he knocks on every open window. He does not give up when he receives retorts from one window; he merely resumes his search for another lead with even more zeal. He tries the hardest to appear and act like a gentleman. Oh, and yes, he does the one task that demands the most courage—he writes poetry!

What, Bau Sahib? You think academics at Bhagwandas is just tomfoolery? No, let me complete what I am saying.

How do you want to study? If you want to become a collector overnight, look for Dubeyji. Rampratap Narayan Dubey. His name is long and so are his sources. Every semester, he spreads a rumour that the papers have definitely been leaked, and after every exam, he throws expletives at his 'reliable source'. Room number 85. Yes, so if you want to be a collector, find Dubeyji. It won't be too expensive; just buy him some tea to stay up all night, and if you want, some bread-pakora from Dilip's shop. Dubeyji will give you such a tablet that all you have to do is vomit it out on your answer sheet. You'll pass, guaranteed.

Tablet! What kind of tablet?

Arre, it's his patent. They say, if everyone buys the pill from him, our country's education problems would be solved! It's called Formula One—the formula of one, which means you read one chapter and write about it in all five questions. Here's the logic: They can ask any kind of question, but a student can write only what he's read. So Dubeyji prepares one answer and attempts all five questions in the exam.

Ohho! You don't just want to pass, you want actual knowledge as well? Oh, you should have told me that before! I told you a whole story for nothing!

Go join Rajiv Pande's class. It is taught in room number 86. He'll teach so well, even professors will suck up to you. After he had exhausted all his UPSC attempts, Pandeji attained enlightenment and came here to study law. He reads voraciously and writes as much as he reads. Often, he can't complete his papers because he doesn't know when to stop writing. So never ask him his score, under any circumstances! He'll lose his head. But our revered scholar can't write his exam if he doesn't get his khaini, his tobacco, in time!

And since you've asked, I'll tell you what B.D. Jeevis think of academics.

Dada: Kenya-Holland match (waste of time).

Rajiv Pande: A representation or rendering of any object or scene intended, not for exhibition as an original work of art, but for the information, instruction or assistance of the maker; as a study of heads or hands for a figure picture.

My god!

Jaivardhan: Ghanta!

Baba: ABCDEFG—A Boy Can Do Everything for Girls.

Dubeyji: Machinery to create servants of the system.

Knowledge is strewn everywhere in Bhagwandas Hostel, you just need someone who can see it. Oh, that reminds me . . .

Do you watch movies, Bau Sahib?

What, really? Few people know as much about movies as you do?

Okay, then tell me, which was the first film Dolly Thakur appeared in?

What? *Dastoor*?

Arre, Bau Sahib. That's why they tell you, figure out the difference between Dolly Thakur and Dolly Minhas before you come to Bhagwandas!

Meet Navenduji in room number 88. He's the one who edited that Bhansaliya's film. Then the Bhansali fellow didn't put his name in the credits and our man made his way here, saying he would study law and file a case. He has an uncle in every district of the country.

Doctor Uncle, Proctor Uncle, Electrician Uncle, Politician Uncle, Horse Uncle, Donkey Uncle. Even if you keep the ubiquitous uncles aside, Navenduji is still an important man. Knows so much about films that he could write a book on *Pakeezah*. He practically has a doctorate in *Sholay*. The size of Amitabh's pants, all about Dhanno's dad, the bullets' exact brand, Basanti's skirt length, he knows it all. *Gabbarva saraisa khaata hai*, you know that whole thing about Gabbar chewing Saraisa tobacco, *haan*? I heard that from him.

Amitabh Bachchan may not remember how many films he's called Vijay in. He would probably say seventeen, but Navendu would reply, 'Hey! You forgot to count *Nisshabd*.' In *Gadar*, when a fly sat on Sunny Deol's nose, Mr Navendu immediately announced that the film would go for the Oscars; anyone can direct a person, but to direct a fly . . . wow! What direction! Such is the genius of Navenduji.

Oh, so the story seems interesting? You want to hear the whole story? Okay, sit down then. This will take a while. Order some chips and a bottle of Pepsi.

Now Bau Sahib, there's no reason for me to be embarrassed in front of you, and since the story must be told, I must tell you at the start, I'm going to be your narrator. Me, as in, Suraj. Yes, yes, him. Girls' hostel and all that. Don't tell anyone! I think of you as my friend, so I'm sharing all this with you.

The story starts after the end of the thirteen-legged coalition government. The tsunami had shown its face and

Bombay, the financial capital of the country, was learning to live amid bomb blasts.

But this story is about the cultural capital, Banaras. And it isn't even about Banaras, Sahib! This is a story about Bhagwandas Hostel, the thirty-sixth hostel of BHU, in the heart of Banaras. The hostel of lawyers.

'Okay, so to go to Bhagwandas Hostel you have to travel to Banaras. Come on, that's the centre of education, isn't it? Banaras Hindu University, which you also call BHU. Come on, let's go . . .'

Aagaaz: The Beginning

Welcome to Banaras Hindu University's Bhagwandas Hostel. If you are among the first sixty students of the country's third-best law college, then Bhagwandas is for you. If not, don't worry! It's for your friends as well. Neither has Bhagwandas itself objected to giving anyone a few days' worth of shelter, nor has its warden, Sadashiv Rao Murali Sir. Among those sixty students are the three of us, the people in this story: Me, that is Suraj, whom my friends call Baba; Anurag aka Dada; and Jaivardhan. How we met is a story in itself.

I needed my father's income certificate during counselling and had forgotten to carry it along with the other certificates. I was told I could not be admitted without it. Now, looking for a father in a new city is like searching for Keshav Paan Bhandar in Canada—too much hassle. I was pacing up and down nervously when my messiah caught sight of me—Anurag De. Smoking a cigarette at the faculty gate, my lord and saviour asked me, 'Something wrong?'

'Haan, bhai, I forgot to bring my father's income certificate. Now they're saying they won't give me admission without it,' I said, wiping the sweat off my brow.

'That's it? That's what has made you this upset? Come on, tell me your father's name,' said Anurag De, taking out a register from his bag.

'Shri Jayant Kishore,' I said, watching him, surprised.

'There you go, here's the signature of Shri Jayant Kishore. It's in Hindi. The job's done. Now, do I have to tell you what to write as well?' he said casually as he signed the paper.

'No, no! I can write it myself but won't that be wrong?' I asked.

'Guru, there's only one thing that's wrong in this world and that's failure. And anyway, it's not like you're making a wrong declaration, are you? You're putting down the income correctly,' he said.

'Thank you. I'll be back after submitting this. By the way, I'm Suraj,' I said.

'And I'm Anurag De.'

'De? A Bengali?' I asked.

He just laughed in reply.

'Can I call you Dada?' I added.

'Call me anything, guru! Your words, your wish. Raja . . . this is Banaras!' Dada said, smiling.

We were still talking when we saw another guy walking around, looking rather worried. He ran first towards the counselling room and then towards the dean's office. Dada stopped him and asked, 'Something wrong?'

'Yeah! I forgot to bring my father's income . . . ' He hadn't even completed his sentence when we burst into laughter. Seeing his confused face, Dada turned towards me and said, 'You go finish your procedure. Meanwhile, I'll tell him the procedure of making up a father.'

'Okay.' As I was leaving, I turned towards the boy and asked, 'My name is Suraj, and yours?'

'Jaivardhan Sharma.'

There's a famous proverb: Birds of a feather flock together. Maybe that's why the three of us met during counselling itself. We were told that our hostel would be Bhagwandas Hostel or B.D. Hostel. Only two people could fit in one room, and Dada offered to be my roommate first. We were allotted room number 79. Jaivardhan hadn't found a roommate yet, so he was temporarily allotted a single room until another student was assigned this hostel.

Bhagwandas Hostel. Legend has it that the hostel was built on the foundations of a prison which dated back to the British era. The geography of it was as such: to its left was Gurtu Hostel for commerce students, and to its right was Radhakrishna Hostel for agricultural students. There was a forest at the back, and, in front, it was fortified by an iron gate. As for political science, it went like this: Bhagwandas had its own unwritten constitution, and following it was just as mandatory as it is for any democracy. Of all the rights, the right to speak freely was used most often. There was no need to get drunk or for Holi revelry to abuse someone. People were called shitheads, assholes and fuckers in a single conversation.

Here, the foremost fundamental duty was to respect your seniors. If a senior passing by was not as tall as you, you had to bend until you were shorter than him and then wait for him to leave. We carried out our duties with utmost dedication and devotion.

We realized that this college wasn't like the ones in romantic films, but what we didn't know was that the first month would be a horror movie. Since our admission, we'd heard that there was no ragging culture in the law faculty. But, as they say in Bhagwandas, hiding knowledge from those who are wise and hiding yourself from the seniors are both impossible tasks. All preparations for our welcome were being made with the stealth of robbers in the night-time. Ragging, in Banarasi, was called *ragad*, or scrub, and it was going to be tested on us that evening itself. Unsuspecting of all this, smoke rings were being blown in room number 79. Dada had just made three continuous smoke rings when someone knocked on the door.

'Who's there?' Dada asked, throwing away his cigarette for fear of the warden.

The knocking became louder in response.

'It's open,' I said, dusting talcum powder around the room to dilute the smell of the smoke. When nobody came in, I thought it was a prank.

'*Abey*, it's Jaivardhanva. He's up to his tricks again,' I told Dada.

'Motherfucker! What is this drama? The door is open, why don't you just enter, huh? Threw my freaking cigarette away because of you,' Dada shouted.

'Suraj and Anurag De. At exactly 6 p.m., fifteen minutes from now, both of you are to be present in the common room. Today is your introduction.' The authoritative voice froze us to our bones.

'Who was that?' I whispered.

'Seniors. Our ragging is about to start,' Dada said softly.

'What? Ragging? But that doesn't happen here, right?' I said, trying to quell my fear.

'Kid, where there are seniors, there's ragging,' Dada said as he put on a T-shirt.

'But it says on the gate that this is an anti-ragging zone!' I snivelled, on the verge of tears.

'It also says on the gate that this is an anti-smoking zone, but we're smoking here, right? Now don't you burst into tears! We'll go calmly. Whatever these people tell us to do, we'll do it bindaas. It's evening, anyway, and we're all just boys in here,' Dada tried to console me.

'I've heard they make you pee on the heater!' My fear was now apparent in my voice.

'Guru, whether they make us pee on the heater or pee a litre, we will have to do it. Let's pray to Bholenath for the best and go. We have to go,' Dada said, opening the door.

When we came out of our room, we were told this *ragdai* had a few rules. There would be a lottery and only five juniors would be ragged in a day. Besides us, the winners of the lottery that day were Jaivardhan Sharma, Navenduji and Rampratap Narayan Dubey or Dubeyji, who were pacing outside impatiently. Navenduji was the one who told us the rules.

'What're they going to ask? Any idea?' Jaivardhan asked this nonsensical question.

'Yeah totally. Data interpretation, reasoning and a little bit of general awareness. Stop talking like a fool,' Dada said.

'They can ask absolutely anything! I've seen it in the movie *Holi*. They can even tell you to walk on the railing! It was Aamir Khan's first film, *Holi*.' Navenduji had started to enlighten us on our first meeting itself.

'Come on! You're giving a walkover even before the match! Just look at Suraj. The poor guy has put on three underpants just listening to these rumours,' Dada said, laughing.

'Okay, let's go now, it's time.' Dubeyji had voiced the most important thing. While walking with him, I noticed that one of his legs was paralysed. This was the first time I had met him.

When we reached the common room, I felt like a traveller without a ticket on seeing the TTE—like a deer stuck in marshy ground when it sees a jackal; like someone unarmed looking at a lathi-bearer. Everything was just as we had imagined. Only one thing was unanticipated—the aroma of food. Smells of spices and flowers. Thinking that maybe it was a tradition to feed juniors after ragging them, I stepped inside the room with my friends. There were exactly ten people inside—ten seniors. It seemed like they had probably smiled last during Kumble's ten-wicket haul. Someone was probably referring to these very people when they said that the difference between a criminal lawyer and a criminal is just of a degree.

'Stand in line according to your height!' a senior thundered.

Dubeyji was right at the front, followed by Jaivardhan and Navenduji, after which there was me and then Dada, who was the tallest of us all.

'What's your name?' another senior asked Dubeyji.

'Rampratap Narayan Dubey,' Dubeyji said, with the air of a soldier reporting to his commanding officer.

'Is this a name or Draupadi's saree? Doesn't freaking finish!' a senior said, suppressing his laughter. 'And your father's name?' he asked.

'Shri Jaikumar Dubey,' Dubeyji answered in the same manner.

'What . . . Jack Dubey? Here I'm asking you your father's name, and you're talking about jacking off, huh! You really want to, don't you? Come, I'll make you jack off, boy. I'll definitely give you something to jack off to,' the senior said harshly.

'No, sir. My father's name *is* Jaikumar Dubey,' Dubeyji whimpered, giving up his soldierly airs.

'Look at this! The son's name is a monkey's tail and the father's name is a complete fail,' quipped a senior who looked easy-going. 'Life has been unfair to you, man. Think about it, a father with such a short name, and his son's name doesn't seem to end. Say, what's been done with you is wrong, isn't it?'

'It is.'

'Then come on, call home and hurl exactly ten expletives at your father.' The senior sounded determined.

'What!' Dubeyji was confounded.

'Yes! Now tell me your residence phone number,' a bearded senior demanded.

'Sir, forgive me. I won't be able to do this,' Dubeyji pleaded.

'Won't be able to? Of course you'll be able to! You're going to be a lawyer; how can you be afraid of grilling another party Quick, give me your phone number,' said the senior, picking up the hostel's landline receiver.

Dubeyji made several pleas but eventually gave them the phone number. All of us had witnessed a trailer of the horror film this was going to be, but Dubeyji was clearly the star of this scene.

'It's ringing. Here, take it. Talk,' a broad-bodied senior said, passing the black receiver to Dubeyji.

Dubeyji did not have an option now. He put the receiver to his ear and started talking.

'Hello, Papaji. *Pranaam*. Yes . . . everything is okay. Yes, the hostel has been assigned. Yes, my studies are also going okay. Listen to me, you wizened old chap. Why in the world did you give me such a long name? Couldn't it have been shorter, like yours? Doesn't even fit in the freaking column when I try to fill out a goddamn form! If I try to book train tickets, it takes so long to fill in the name that I end up on the waiting list! Is it a name or an organic chemistry formula? Everyone calls me RPND here. First there was DDT and now there's RPND! But how would that even matter to you? You just sit with four men, idle as a bone, discussing everything from vegetable rates to election dates. What is it, have you been roughed up? Is that why you're not saying anything, huh? You sure had a lot to say when I wanted to become a CA. Remember what you said? That if I wanted to do anything, I had better do a BA, because B comes before C! Once a dimwit, always a dimwit! Anyway, I'll hang up now. I'm your son, do forgive me. Pranaam, Papaji.'

Dubeyji put the phone down and after a deep breath, he looked towards the seniors. All of them clapped for him.

'Well done! You've made a stellar argument just like a true lawyer! Just one problem: there weren't exactly ten expletives. Anyway, never mind, your class is over. Go now, count the white hair in that man's beard,' a senior said, gesturing towards the bearded senior. Dubeyji silently moved towards him.

Everyone's eyes were now on Jaivardhan.

'You, come forward. What's your name?'

'Jaivardhan.'

'Jaivardhan what?'

'Jaivardhan Sharma.'

'Sharma! Where from? I mean, where do you live?'

'From Patna.' Jaivardhan was starting to feel a little comfortable.

'Where in Patna?' The senior was growing even more curious.

'Ashiyanagar,' Jaivardhan replied, as if he were saying he lived in Los Angeles.

'Somewhere near Rajabazaar?' the senior asked, becoming more and more inquisitive by the second.

'Abey, what are you going in so deep for? Do you want to get your cousin married to him or what?' shouted the senior who was getting his beard hair counted.

'You idiot, you keep mum . . . you're letting the country's future generation count your beard hairs and you're the one who wants to speak up?' the senior said before turning to Jaivardhan again. 'Yes, so, somewhere near Rajabazaar?'

'Yes, to the right of Rajabazaar.'

'Guru, why didn't you tell me before? You're from Jawaari! Come, come, sit down. Rakesh, bring some sweet rabri! This guy's turned out to be my neighbour! Hey man, everything all right in Patna?' the senior asked as he helped Jaivardhan into a chair.

As he sat, Jaivardhan looked at us as if he had pulled some sort of a jugaad and would certainly be able to get them to cut us some slack.

'Everything is all right in Patna,' Jaivardhan said as if he were the chief minister of Bihar. 'Here, have some rabri, tell us, how did you end up here?' a senior said, taking some sweets and handing them to Jaivardhan.

'I don't eat sweets.' By now, Jaivardhan had also forgotten that seniors had to be addressed as 'Sir'.

'Oh no, these aren't sweets, are they? They're Baba Bholenath's prasad, holy offerings! You're in Banaras now, this is the land of Bhole Baba! Consider them holy and eat,' the senior said kindly.

The meaning of Baba Bholenath's prasad was simple—bhaang, the cannabis preparation characteristic of Banaras. This euphemism wasn't a cryptic puzzle for Banarasis.

Whoever wanted some accepted it politely and whoever didn't denied it even more politely. There was no pressure. Pressure was never a defining feature of Banaras, but this was useful only to those who knew the defining features of Banaras in the first place. Those who hadn't been there even for a full fortnight would take some time to get familiar with the local lingo. Jaivardhan was one of these people. It was a trap and Jaivardhan had been caught in it.

'I'll eat it if you say so,' Jaivardhan replied, eating a spoonful of rabri.

'Okay, now that you're here, answer a couple of questions or everyone will accuse me of regionalism.'

'Yes, Sir, go for it!' Jaivardhan had eaten half the bowl by now.

'So . . . why does the king of Banaras have his palace outside Banaras?' the senior asked, reading Jaivardhan's expressions.

'I . . . I . . . I don't know, Sir.' Jaivardhan had eaten the entire bowl. His throat was starting to get parched.

'Because the emperor of Banaras is Bholenath, and there can't be two emperors in one place, so the king of Kashi has his palace across the Ganga, in Ramnagar. Got it?' the senior explained.

'Ye . . . s . . . I mea . . . can I get some water please . . .?' Jaivardhan had started to stutter.

'Yes, you can get some water. First answer this: Who commissioned Vishwanath Temple?' The senior was laughing cruelly. All the other seniors had now started to gather around Jaivardhan.

'I don't know. Wa . . . wat . . . water please,' Jaivardhan was getting shifty now. He was thirsty—normal before the effects of bhaang kick in.

'Ahilyabai Holkar,' the senior said. 'Okay, now this is your last question. Look, definitely answer this one, it's a question of Patna's honour! Tell me, where is Vishwanath Temple?'

'For all I care it could be in your dad's backyard! You asshole, I've been asking for water and you're throwing questions at me?' Jaivardhan exploded.

This sudden onset of the bhaang's effects threw the seniors off at first, but then they started to enjoy the situation. The motive of feeding him bhaang was, after all, to enjoy the situation. The drug was doing its job well. Jaivardhan started looking for water as soon as he got off the chair. After drinking half of the bottle kept in a corner of the common room, he said, 'You love asking questions, don't you? Should I ask questions? Tell me, you asshole, did Akbar eat onions?'

Rather than answering his question, the seniors started to laugh. This was how Jaivardhan was being ragged, but how was he to understand that in his situation? He was murmuring to himself: 'Asking questions, are you? Go shove this stupid shit up your arse. Spent two weeks in Banaras and the fuckers have started calling themselves Banarasi. Called them "Sir" a couple of times and now they're just spoilt rotten. If I hadn't wasted two years preparing for the Probationary Officer exam, I would have been your senior and I would have been giving you a freaking hard time.

Won't give me water, huh? Listen, you, there were fellows like you back in Saidpur Hostel who used to fill water for me, and salute me thrice a day on top of that.'

Jaivardhan was acting more and more roguish by the second.

'So, you gave me some rabri, and you think you bought me off? Do you think I'm your slave now? Well, here's the truth, I'm not.'

'Careful . . . careful. Abusing us isn't a good idea,' teased a senior.

'Abusing? So, you people are incapable of tolerating some abuses now? You idiots, you don't know how to walk your talk. You're all bark and no bite, that's what you are!'

Jaivardhan had reached that point of being high where his speech was no longer being controlled by his mind. His words were getting caught in his tongue. The good part was that the bhaang didn't make him wreak any more havoc. He had started to fall asleep. Saying 'all bark and no bite' over and over, he finally passed out from exhaustion.

As soon as he fell, he was put on some sacks in a corner of the common room. His ragad was over. Next up was one of the three of us.

'You, French cut, come here.' It was Navenduji's turn. He adjusted his clothes as if he were going for an interview and then approached the senior.

'Tell me about your hobbies.'

'Sir, I'm interested in dalteology.'

'What? Come again? Wow, what a talented batch of people has joined this year! One's talking about jacking off, the other's talking about dallying and dalliances!' said the senior, seventy-seven hairs of whose beard Dubeyji had counted.

'Sir, I like to collect postcards. That's called dalteology.'

'That is deltiology, you idiot! Anyway, it's good to know that you're interested in collecting.'

'Thank you, Sir,' said Navenduji, heaving a sigh of relief. He had cited this hobby on purpose. He thought there was nothing anyone could possibly ask about a hobby like this.

'Okay, then here's what you can do. Go collect a book from one of your friend's rooms, without him knowing you took it. And remember, your friend should be in the room! That's when you will be considered a successful collector. I will come with you till the room,' the senior announced, setting the rules.

'But, Sir, that would be stealing, right?' Navenduji asked nervously.

'What, so are you not planning to return the book tomorrow? A thief, is that what you are?' the senior snapped.

'Sorry, Sir.'

'Okay then, let's go quickly. And be back in ten minutes,' he ordered.

Navenduji, a saintly man. His name was suffixed by 'ji' only because he never discriminated against anyone when it came to paying them respect—be it plants or animals, living creatures or non-living creatures, professors or students. Forget saying cuss words out aloud, he couldn't even write them down. He hadn't even called an actual ass an ass. Overall, our Navenduji wasn't very different from Hiraman from *Teesri Kasam*.

Today, this man had to steal. Thinking to himself that both Bhagwan and Bhagwandas were watching him, Navenduji entered Sushil's room, which was the closest to the common room.

When Navenduji tiptoed in, Sushil was sleeping with a blanket over his face. Navenduji went quietly to his table. A lamp was lit and, other than books, there was a photo frame with a picture of a girl in it. It was clear from the photo that this was Sushil's sister. After taking a look at the photograph, Navenduji picked up the slimmest book he could see and put it inside his shirt. He was just about to head out when he heard Sushil's voice: 'Navenduji? What are you doing?'.

'I was looking for your family album,' Navenduji said calmly, sounding admirably unperturbed. He turned around and sat on the bed.

'My family album? Why?' Sushil replied, sounding part confused and part annoyed.

'Wanted to match her face. Your sister's. She's gorgeous, she really is!' Navenduji said, weighing his words.

'What?' Sushil was astounded.

'Yes! I'm not lying. Whom does she look like though, uncle or aunty?' Navenduji was a saintly man. Of course he never lied.

'What do you mean? Don't you have any manners? I'll complain about you to the warden tomorrow itself!' Sushil shouted.

'Come on, I was just giving her a compliment. It's all right if you don't want the compliment, but Sushilji, please don't be offended.'

'Get out of here!' Sushil screamed.

'Yes, yes, I'm going, but there's just one thing, Sushilji. This is the age to put up your girlfriend's photos, and if you sit around with your sister's photos, then these things are bound to happen, right? Now if this was your girlfriend's photo . . . '

'Just get out!' Sushil yelled.

'There was a similar case of confusion in the film *Insaaf Main Karoonga*. It happened with Rajesh Khanna when . . .' Navenduji hadn't even finished imparting his knowledge when Sushil bellowed, 'Just get out at once!'

'I'm going, Sushilji, but listen, please don't worry yourself thinking about all this,' said Navenduji, expressing his concern.

'My dear friend, please, please get out of my room,' said Sushil, folding his hands.

Navenduji could not bear to see anyone crying. When he was convinced that Sushil would fall at his feet if he did not leave right then, he walked out. He had planned to come back and talk to Sushil after giving the book to the senior, but Sushil slammed the door shut the moment he left. Navenduji gave the book to the senior and went back to the recreation room with him. His ragging was over.

The next would either be Dada or me. But it was not one of us, but both of us together. Maybe that's why we had been called at the end.

'Room number 79, come forward,' an order thundered. Both of us went up to the issuer of this order. By then, the seniors had clustered together around us.

'Both of you have written your names on your room door. Is the door your personal property?' a voice capable of striking fear into any heart echoed in the room.

'Sorry, Sir,' I said, staring at my shirt's third button. I had read somewhere that you should keep looking at your shirt's third button when you are being ragged. It gives a good impression.

'So, both of you smoke cigarettes?' the bearded senior asked. 'No, Sir,' I replied.

'Yes, Sir,' Dada said.

'Why do you smoke?' The question was directed to Dada.

'Eighty-four per cent of the world's literate people smoke and I don't want to be illiterate,' came Dada's quick reply.

'Okay, so that means you consider yourself literate?' sneered the senior.

'I am literate,' Dada replied confidently.

'Very daring, aren't you? Then your task should also demand some daring. What do you say, guys?' the senior asked his fellows. After much discussion among them, a task was finally given to us, and it wasn't less than suicide.

'Yes! So, room number 79, this task is for both of you. You will enter the girls' hostel and bring back any one item which only girls use,' said the senior, hiding a knowing smile.

'What? Girls' hostel?' I was stunned. I hadn't imagined this even in my wildest dreams.

'But, Sir, the girls' hostel is like a fort. It's impossible to enter it!' said Dada, as if he would have agreed to this task had it been possible.

'That is not your concern. Durga Maharaj, the cook from our mess, will get you into the hostel. After that, the responsibility is yours.'

'Sir, I don't agree to this ta . . . ' I had barely finished the sentence when a benumbing slap left my ears devoid of any sensation.

'Don't agree? Do you think we're trying to pass a bill here? Who asked for your opinion? Fucker . . . give you an inch and here you are trying to take a mile. Shut up, go and return fast. And remember, something which only girls use! If you bring some nonsense or come back without anything, then we'll send you again, and this time you'll have to get in by yourself.'

'But, Sir, how will we get in?' asked Dada.

'I told you, Durga Maharaj will take you inside. Durga . . . drop them to Triveni Hostel. Don't come back till they return!' the senior told the cook.

Durga Maharaj, Bhagwandas Hostel's cook. Every cook here is called Maharaj. To sustain his position in the hostel amid immense competition, Durga Maharaj too had no option but to obey the seniors. It was possible that when we became seniors the following year, Durga Maharaj would have to deal with us as well. He was just functioning according to the laws of nature.

Anyway, Durga Maharaj and the two started walking towards Triveni Hostel. The girls' hostel was about a kilometre away from Bhagwandas Hostel. Durga Maharaj kept explaining the dos and don'ts along the way.

'Here, keep this towel around your neck, only then you will look like cooks, no? If someone asks, you say you are Durga's nephew. The didis, if they say things, don't be angry. Then everything will go wrong. Different didis think differently, no? Take this polythene. You need to bring an item na, will be easy to carry,' Maharaj said with a smile.

'Can't you walk quietly?' I snapped.

'Arre, I was saying for your good only. Everything will go wrong if you are caught in checking when you come outside,' Durga Maharaj replied, offended.

After that, Durga Maharaj said nothing the whole way. Neither of us said anything either. I could guess the purpose of this task. The more I tried to stop thinking about it, the more it kept coming to my mind. Before I could separate myself from these thoughts, we were at Triveni Hostel's gate. The gatekeeper recognized Durga Maharaj. After a few greetings, Durga said, 'These two people . . . from my village. Now they will work here, with Kedar Maharaj.'

'All right, get their names noted,' said the gatekeeper.

'Come, how will this writing names help? Who knows if they will even last two days or no. Write their names tomorrow. Go, go work now. Kedar is an angry man, be careful when you work,' said Durga, gesturing us to step inside.

A strange shiver ran up my body the moment I entered. Technically the accommodation for the mess staff was different from the hostel, but I was still shitting myself with fear. I was just about to hide my face with the towel when Dada said, grinding his teeth, 'What are you doing? If you tie up your face in this heat, you'll start looking suspicious.'

'Bhai, I'm afraid.'

'So am I, but what can we do? Should we go to the gatekeeper and tell him that bhai, we're not here to carry utensils, we're here to carry away girls' things,' Dada said angrily.

'So, what do we do?'

'You don't do anything. Just come with me.'

'What will we carry, bhai? I mean, what are we going to take?' I asked, walking with him.

'As if you don't know,' whispered Dada.

In our T-shirts and hosiery lowers, we didn't look any different from the mess staff. The towel on our shoulders helped us fit in completely. Nobody doubted us among mess workers, more so because new faces were often seen at the mess mid-session. We had managed to get into the mess penthouse asking for Kedar Maharaj, but our motive wasn't to meet him. Our actual goal was to somehow enter the girls' hostel. We made our way through onions, potatoes and peas and finally reached the mess. There was chaos in there. I had seen so many girls together only in movies, those dance sequences. Everyone was talking, nobody was listening. Perhaps Dada was thinking about something, but

I was too busy admiring the girls. Suddenly, my wandering gaze paused at a bench.

'Dada . . . Dada . . . Look there. Abey, those are girls from our faculty. I've seen them in our faculty!'

'Then, bhai, you can see them again in the faculty. Did we take so much risk so you could look at girls from our own faculty?' Dada hissed.

'Did you think of anything?' I asked, looking down.

'Yes. We'll have to wait for the girls to eat and then go up. Then we'll cross this small passageway and enter their corridor. We'll probably find something or the other there, outside.' Dada sounded hopeful.

'All right, but what should we do until then?'

'You stare at the girls. I'll sit here and shell peas.'

Dada truly was my best friend.

By the time the girls left, Dada had shelled about two kilos of peas, and I had memorized the faces of at least two dozen girls. I was just thinking about the twenty-fifth when Dada interrupted my thoughts, 'Have all of them gone?'

'Yes.'

'Then why aren't you telling me, fucker? Have we come here to shell peas?' Dada said angrily.

'Bhai, I was thinking about how lucky the mess workers are! Sure, the girls all call them bhaiya, but how does that matter? Even Paro used to call Devdas "Devdas Da" in the film right?' I cursed my luck.

'Okay, blabber later, listen carefully now . . . I will cross this passageway and hopefully find something in the corridor. You handle the mess staff until then, okay?' Dada explained.

'All right, but Dada, wait a couple of minutes. I'll just be back from the bathroom.'

'Oh, god!' Dada said, irritated. 'I had asked you to look at girls, not to fantasize about them!'

'No, yaar. It's not like that. I really need to pee.'

'How wonderful! Possibly for the first time in the history of BHU, two people have entered the girls' hostel. And why have they done it? To take a piss!' Dada snapped.

'Have you seen the bathroom anywhere?' I asked, trying to stop the argument.

'I didn't see it on the way here. Okay, look over there. See that hall thing next to the mess? Maybe that's the washroom or a bathroom. Rush there and come back quickly. We need to complete the task and return.'

The washroom was about a hundred metres from the mess. I entered it quickly, closed my eyes and started to relieve myself. I jumped when I opened my eyes and saw my own face staring back at me. There was a little mirror in front of me. Girls have mirrors even in their washrooms. I think our whole hostel had half a mirror combined. With this thought, I was just about zip up my pants and leave, when I suddenly saw an 'object' kept on the mirror stand. My legs began to tremble. My heart started pounding. I quickly pressed that 'object' into my fist and ran towards Dada.

'Guru, the job's done!'

'Yes, your expression says that,' remarked Dada.

'Not that, the other job!'

'Really, what did you find? Where is it?' Dada asked eagerly.

'In my fist.'

'In your fist? Taking things in your fist now,' Dada said, with an obscene hand gesture. 'Anyway, you're a class apart. Capable of absolutely anything. Now quick, show me what you have got, ' he said impatiently.

'Look!' I opened my fist.

'Lipstick!'

'Yes! Lipstick!' I said happily.

'You idiot, what is this nonsense you've got? We needed . . . ' Dada paused.

'Yes, go on! Come on, tell me! Which boy uses this, huh? Only girls use this!' I explained.

'*Jiyo kareja*! Heaven bless you, kid! You've won me over! First smart thing you've done in all these days!'

'Okay then, let's leave,' I said. The only way out was the gate we had come in from, but we were a little less afraid now. When we were leaving, the gatekeeper asked, 'Where are you going now?'

'To get hing. Didis of this hostel, they don't eat dal without hing only,' Dada said, imitating Durga Maharaj, and we came out laughing.

As soon as we left, we saw Durga Maharaj standing on guard, waiting for us. The seniors wanted to make sure that we didn't step out of the hostel and buy something from the shops. Durga Maharaj's face lit up when he saw us. After walking for a while, he came up from behind and asked, 'Found anything?'

I didn't reply and said to Dada, 'Our task was the most difficult.'

'Would you have abused your father?' Dada asked.

'No, man,' I said, softly.

'Then? All you do is talk nonsense.'

'Bro, maybe the seniors will see the lipstick and get annoyed, and then they'll give us something else to do,' I said doubtfully.

'And maybe if we took something else, they would have asked us for lipstick.'

'Hmm . . .'

As soon as we entered the hostel, Durga Maharaj overtook us and escorted us to the common room, where all the seniors were waiting. Navenduji and Dubeyji were trying to wake Jaivardhan up. When we reached, a senior asked, 'Is the job done?'

'Yes,' Dada replied.

'Then come on, show us. Come here guys, let's look at some explosive material.'

'Here you go,' Dada said, handing him the lipstick.

'What's this now? A lipstick?'

'Yes, boys won't use this, will they?' Dada had just said this much when the seniors burst into laughter. Some patted our backs, some shook our hands. After joking around for a bit, a senior said to Dada, 'You're a witty guy, kid. I'm sure you'll make it big.'

'Thank you, Sir,' Dada and I chorused. Everyone shook hands with all four of us again and then the bearded senior said, 'It was a pleasure meeting all of you. Welcome to BHU. Welcome to Law School. Enjoy the journey—it's called the golden phase of life. If you have any issues, personal or academic, don't hesitate to approach us. Every senior will help you as much as they can. No hard feelings. No personal bias. Everything done here was just to break the ice between us. Okay, then, all of you can go now. And remember, you are not to discuss the tasks given here with anyone else, because their ragad is still left. And one more thing, if any faculty member asks about ragging, then you know what you have to say, clear?'

'Yes, Sir,' all four of us said together.

'Arre, listen! Go, put your friend to bed in his room,' the senior said, referring to Jaivardhan. Saying 'Yes, Sir,' Dada and I lifted Jaivardhan by his shoulders. Navenduji and Dubeyji followed.

'How did you guys get this thing?' Navenduji asked.

'Don't even ask, Navenduji. We just thank our lucky stars at this point,' I replied.

'Those people made me steal! The lowliest deed of all. Tomorrow morning I will go apologize to both Bholenath and Sushilnath,' Navenduji said, eyeing Sushil's door.

'I got the easiest task, I was safe,' Dubeyji said.

'Of course, you ass! Has there ever been anything easier than hurling abuses at your father?' Dada said, putting Jaivardhan on his bed.

'Which father? Whose father? Just because I gave the correct name, you think I gave the correct phone number? Seniors like these lick my effing boots,' Dubeyji finished his sentence with a clever smile, leaving us astounded. It was not so easy to comprehend this man.

* * *

Getting through ragging was like completing a life sentence. Seniors made the environment friendly by throwing us a freshers' party and assuring us of any kind of help. Dada, Jaivardhan and I were favoured by the seniors after the ragging. We were close to each other as well and always seen together. Like all other Bengalis, Dada's love for cigarettes had been bequeathed to him by his ancestors—a cultural heritage. So, after breakfast at the mess, the next step was Panditji's paan shop, which was the centre of all kinds of debates.

'Books are too expensive, man!' Dada said.

'And cigarettes are dirt cheap, aren't they?' I replied.

'Don't compare cigarettes to books! If there were no cigarettes, these books wouldn't even get written. They're a stress buster.' Dada blew a smoke ring.

'Ghanta he'll get how cigarettes work! The guy just started smoking. Keeps the smoke in his mouth, blows it out and thinks he's a superhero, Arjun Rampal or something. This is the kind of guy who brings shame to cigarettes,' Jaivardhan said, taking the cigarette from Dada.

'Okay, forget cigarettes, tell me, which books should we buy?' Dada asked.

'Why don't we consult some lecturers?' I suggested.

'You're spewing bullshit again, you dumb fuck. What will a lecturer tell you? He's read one book his whole life and he's still reading it. We have to study ten subjects here!' Jaivardhan said.

'All right then, let's go to Animesh Bhaiya. He's a good senior, he'll tell us which book is good,' I opined.

'Yes, you ass. The guy hyped you up, told you that you sound like an intellectual and now he's a good senior! Can't you see that the idiot has been wearing your jacket for the past five days? If you go to ask him about books, he'll make you take off your shirt as well. Jump from the frying pan and you'll land in the fire.' We were slowly getting familiar with Jaivardhan's idioms and proverbs.

'Idiots, you'll never reach a decision. All right, let's buy three books each. We don't need a book for Professional Ethics. Okay?' Dada asked.

'All right,' I said.

'Yeah, okay,' Jaivardhan agreed.

'And what about Bare Act?' I asked.

'Again with the dirty talk! Don't say all these gross bare-share things during study time!' Jaivardhan laughed.

* * *

The minimum requirement for an LLB three-year course is graduation. We were all graduates, but who attends classes in college? We weren't used to classes any more. Now, attending five classes a day was a pain in the neck.

We had to study ten subjects, and 75 per cent attendance was mandatory in each class.

'What kind of a college is this? We didn't study ten subjects in six months even when we were in school!' I remarked.

'Who said this is a college? It's literally called a law school; 75 per cent attendance is compulsory,' said Jaivardhan.

'Who told you?' I asked.

'How did you pass the exam, *bey*? Fucker hasn't even looked at the prospectus. Someone else definitely took his exam for him,' Dada said to Jaivardhan.

'How will I manage the attendance? I was getting so sleepy today, on the first day itself. How will I sit there for five hours every day?' I asked.

'Proxy. It's the only way,' Dada said.

'Even then, how many classes can someone stand proxy for?' Jaivardhan asked.

'We won't need it for all our classes. I've asked the seniors. We'll use proxy only for those classes where the teacher is very strict about attendance. We'll figure out the rest,' Dada said.

'Well then, that's that. I'm tired now, been going to classes all morning. Let's go to Lanka, near Heritage Hospital. I've heard their mango shake is quite good,' Jaivardhan said.

* * *

The lectures went on from 10 a.m. to 5 p.m., six days a week. Teachers were more tied up than the students. The pressure to finish the syllabus in just five months was more on them than it was on us, so classes never got cancelled.

'See, in Hindu Law, there is a probability of questions being repeated, and for short notes, an even greater chance of being repeated,' Professor Abhay Kumar said, flipping through Paras Diwan's book.

(Paras Diwan and Abhay Kumar had a symbiotic relationship. Abhay Kumar was never seen without Paras Diwan's book, and before Abhay Kumar, nobody knew who Paras Diwan was. Abhay Kumar was also connected to 'being'. He hardly ever completed a sentence without saying 'being'.)

'So, the topic being studied yesterday was "marriage". Can anyone answer, what are the essentials of Hindu marriage?' Abhay Kumar asked the class and started looking around for an answer.

'Keep making eye contact, he won't ask us,' I said to Dada softly.

'Abey, he'll definitely ask if we make eye contact,' Dada replied.

'He'll catch you if you avoid his glance. Show some confidence,' I whispered back.

'All right! You, blue shirt! What are the essentials of Hindu marriage?' Abhay Kumar had found his victim.

I looked first at my shirt, then at Dada's, then heaved a sigh of relief. Neither of our shirts was blue.

'Haven't got the foggiest clue,' came a voice from behind.

Everyone turned and looked. But nobody had the courage to laugh in Abhay Kumar's class.

'What nonsense are you being talking?' Abhay Kumar shouted.

'Yo, it's your job to tell me this stuff, isn't it?' came the reply, with the same confidence.

This time, Abhay Kumar couldn't control himself. The whole class started laughing and so did Abhay Kumar.

'Why . . . what's your name?' he asked.

'Roshan Chaudhuri.' There was stress on every syllable of the name, as if he were reading out a royal title.

Abhay Kumar could do nothing but stare at him. He asked Roshan to leave the class and then resumed teaching.

* * *

Roshan Chaudhuri. I had seen him for the first time during counselling; he was arguing relentlessly with the warden to get a hostel room. The problem was that only one other student could be admitted into the hostel, on merit, and another boy was in the same position as him according to merit. Roshan was adamant that the room be allotted to him because he was older. It was as if his motive wasn't to study but to get the room, and if he didn't get it, he wouldn't take admission at all. The other boy gave up and withdrew his name, so Roshan ultimately got the room. If there was anyone who could match his intellectual capacity in the hostel, it was Navenduji. Whether it be the Cancun Summit or a free-trade permit, Fidel Castro or a music maestro, these were the only two who were aware of all this and knew all the solutions. One Sunday in Bhagwandas

Hostel's official community hall, room number 79, Navenduji was explaining:

'Listen, Surajji. You know the Chaudhari fellow, right? The idiot's a gem of a person. Does this guy even need a sphere of knowledge? When he starts talking on any subject, it feels like you could just listen all day. Just like my uncle in Munger. I mean when he started talking about Article 370, I was wondering what Varmaji would even teach. He remembers 171 cases, knows the entire Minority Commission report by heart. He's completely impressed me, but the poor guy has ended up with a bad roommate,' Navenduji said.

'But doesn't he live alone in room number 68?' I asked.

'No, bro. His roommate has arrived.'

'Three months later? How did he manage to get the hostel?' I asked two questions at once.

'I've heard that he got the hostel allotted beforehand, and he's some judge's son. Name is Shashank.' Navenduji answered a third question as well.

'If your conference is over, can we go to the mess now? It's 2 p.m. and I'm really hungry. If we go late we'll get nothing but dal,' Dada said, imparting his invaluable pearls of wisdom. It was difficult to get food if you were late on Sundays. The three of us got up, locked the room and proceeded towards the mess. But only the fortunate are destined for food. We were just on our way when a voice called from behind us,' Navendruji, Navendruji!'

When we turned to look, there was no one there.

'Someone's calling me,' Navenduji said.

'No, he's calling Navendru. Who's this Navendru now?' I asked.

'Anju Mahendru's brother. Now shut up and come along.' Dada was still hoping to get some dal. But now, even dal was not in our fate. The same muffled voice called out again, 'Navendruji, Navendruji!'

Navenduji and Superman had one similarity. If anyone asked for help, both lost their appetite. Navenduji ran in the direction of the voice. A little investigation revealed that it was coming from the window of room number 68. The door was locked from outside. Roshan Chaudhuri was inside and he was the one calling from the window in a muffled voice.

'Roshanji, you? How did you enter after locking the door from outside?' Navendu asked stupidly.

'First open the door, then I'll tell you.' Roshan sounded scared.

'Navenduji opened the door and Roshan hurried outside.

'What happened?' Navenduji asked.

'My roommate, my roommate!' Roshan was still petrified.

'What the hell happened to your roommate?' Dada's hunger was getting to his head now.

'My roommate makes spirit calls!' Roshan was sweating.

'What?' Navenduji and Dada understood what they had heard. I did not.

'Spirit call? What's that supposed to mean?' I asked.

Dada interrupted, 'Mr Suraj, this is Airtel's new plan, which allows you to make calls from B.D. Hostel to the girls' hostel for just 30 paise! Even Navenduji's uncle . . . '

'Please be quiet, all of you! Can't you see what a serious matter this is?' Navenduji scolded.

'But what are spirit calls?' I asked again.

'Summoning spirits . . . ' replied Navenduji.

'What?' It was my turn to be shocked now.

'Yes! Spirit calls means calling spirits.' Navenduji was looking grave. After a moment of silence, he asked Roshan, 'But how do you know your roommate does all this? And who closed the door?'

'Here, take, read it yourself.' He handed Navenduji a sheet of a paper. Navenduji's expression seemed to change with every word that he read. He was not able to say anything out loud. The same thing happened to Dada when he snatched the sheet and read it. He slowly passed the paper to me.

Indra's daughter has arrived
She is dressed just like a bride
Her braid is longer than her body
And all she eats is kheer and roti
Behold this woman, behold her forehead
Vermillion painted and a dark blood red.

I don't know why but my legs froze as soon as I read it. Nobody was in a state to say anything. Just then, Roshan pointed towards his wall. It had sooty claw prints and something written in an unfamiliar language.

Navenduji broke the silence, 'Who's written this?'

'Shashank, my roommate. He's the one who locked the door from the outside.' Roshan was breathless.

'But where is Shashank?' I asked.

'I don't know. He was muttering something at this paper, then got up suddenly, locked the door from outside and . . .'

Roshan was still explaining when suddenly we heard a scream from somewhere near the bathroom. There were people gathered there. Navenduji had vanished from our side and become part of the crowd. We were going to find out what had happened when we saw Jaivardhan coming from the direction of the bathroom.

'Abey, what happened? Why is there a crowd?' Dada asked.

'What could happen? Some fucker collapsed in the bathroom like a stack of books.' Jaivardhan's sleep had been disturbed. We were still talking when the din from the bathroom got louder. We ran to see what was causing it; the boy was none other than Shashank. Shashank Agarwal. He was lying unconscious on the bathroom floor.

'Bro, what's coming out of his mouth?' Navenduji asked.

'And where's the smell of kerosene coming from?' I asked.

'Fucking hell! This guy's made a suicide attempt!' Dada said, taking his nose closer to Shashank's mouth.

'Listen! Does anyone have his home phone number?' Navenduji asked.

'What a genius you are, Navenduji! Friendship with a fool is as useless as a cloud-covered moon. It's not been even twenty-four hours since he came. We don't even know his name and you're asking for his phone number? Do I look like his brother-in-law? Why would I have his number? Okay, let's go tell Murali Sir first,' Jaivardhan exclaimed angrily.

Every hostel definitely has some students who take everything that happens in the hostel—good, bad, said, unsaid, beautiful, ugly, everything—to the warden. They have only one motive—to be the warden's pet. I didn't know who did that in Bhagwandas, but the news had already reached Murali Sir.

'What be happening here? All you crowding around, poor boy, he die without oxygen. Come on, move, let fresh air come in,' Murali Sir said. He immediately gestured to Navenduji. 'Navendu! This be Shashank's residence number. This number have to be called and someone be asked to come immediately.'

Navenduji quickly snatched Dada's phone and started dialling the number. It connected at once.

'Namaskar, Uncle. Is this Shashank's father? Uncle, this is Navendu speaking from BHU Shashank is my classmate. Both of us live in the same hostel.'

'Navenduji, you don't have to give an interview! Get to the point quickly or the man will take off!' Jaivardhan snapped.

'Huh . . . yes, yes.' Navenduji controlled himself. 'Uncle! Shashank is lying here unconscious.'

The person on the other end of the line said something and Navenduji cut the call.

'You hung up? What happened?' I asked.

'Oh my god! Was that his dad or the devil! He said Shashank is in depression. Will be all right soon. Today won't be possible, he'll be here tomorrow,' Navenduji said, wiping sweat from his brow.

'He's not in depression, he's into some kind of black magic. That's what he was doing when he fainted,' Roshan said.

'Ghanta he does black magic. Do you think he came here to the bathroom to do black magic? That too covered in kerosene?' Jaivardhan asked.

Before the argument could go any further, Murali Sir got up from Shashank's side and approached us. He looked at each of us suspiciously before saying to Navenduji, 'Yes, Navendu. Any luck with the phone call?'

'Sir, I spoke to his dad . . . I mean his father. He said that Shashank is in depression. He'll come tomorrow and take him home,' Navenduji said.

'Yes, even I be thinking that. He be coming to his senses now, take him to his room. Make sure nobody be disturbing him till his father comes and he not try to do this again.' Murali Sir passed on the responsibility to Navenduji.

'Sir, Roshan will be alone in his room when Shashank leaves, so please shift him with Jaivardhan. Jaivardhan was saying he gets lonely without a roommate,' Navenduji said, jumping at the opportunity.

'No, Rajiv Pande isn't getting along with his roommate. We have to be shifting him with Roshan now. We'll think about Jaivardhan later,' Murali Sir said before leaving. Then commenced the operation to take Shashank back to his room.

'Let's lift him up,' I said to Dada, Jaivardhan and Navenduji.

'You seem very worried about me?' Jaivardhan asked Navenduji.

'You live alone. I thought you must be lonely, that's why I asked,' Navenduji said, lifting up Shashank.

'The farmer is at the hoe and you're singing praises of the winnow! If I need anything, I will let you know. You don't have to worry about me,' Jaivardhan retorted.

The four of us lifted Shashank and took him to his bed. Navenduji stayed there, but we left the room because of the smell of kerosene and the creepy sketch.

'Did you find something odd about that room?' I asked Jaivardhan.

'Something! From the room to its occupants, everything seemed odd. God knows what was written there. And how did kerosene even reach the room?' Jaivardhan answered.

'No bey, there was something else too.'

'What?' Dada interrupted.

'There were three pressure cookers in the room,' I said.

'Yes, so one of them must be Shashank's,' Dada replied.

'But if food is served at the mess, then what do you need pressure cookers for? And Shashank just arrived yesterday,' I replied.

'Maybe he cooks vegetarian food in one, chicken-mutton in another and the third for when Roshan Chaudhuri fasts. You have a problem with any of that?' Dada snapped. 'I anyway didn't get lunch because of these crazy fuckers and now you guys are making matters worse by talking about pressure cookers. Now we probably won't get anything even at Hindustan Hotel. Let's catch a rickshaw and go to Lanka,' Dada told Jaivardhan.

'*Ae samaan*! You gonna take us to Lanka?' Jaivardhan stopped a rickshaw driver.

* * *

Although Rajiv Pande is not the main character of this story, he is an important one. Rajiv Pande was among the nerds and Bhagwandas Hostel had some hopes from him. But he had started behaving suspiciously these past few days. He would suddenly stop walking and start counting something on his fingers; he would break a piece of roti in the mess, then keep it there and leave; whenever he heard the radio outside anyone's room, he would just stand there. Rajiv really didn't know what his problem was. Sometimes he was upset because he was too short, sometimes because he wore glasses and sometimes for no reason at all.

According to his roommate, however, his behaviour wasn't suspicious just hilarious. In his room, he would suddenly start reading out poetry from his law textbooks. Occasionally he would also ask the meaning of love. This frustrated his roommate, who eventually requested the warden for a change of room. I was Rajiv's only friend in Bhagwandas Hostel because I understood poetry. Rajiv thought people who understood poetry would also understand love, so he told me that he was in love with Megha.

It was a love so deep that the beloved did not even know about it. In the dictionary of Bhagwandas Hostel, these were called satellite love cases. Often, in love stories such as these, the girl asked the boy for the notes of a class she had missed. From that day on, the boy became Shakespeare, wondering why, of all the people in the universe, she had chosen him. The boy suddenly felt like he had grown up. He got offended when the girl talked to others and even started worrying about her fashion sense. The best part was that the girl was not aware of any of this. She, on the other hand, circulated the notes among her friends and they even found grammatical mistakes in it together. When her friends teased her about him, she rejected his love and his worth with just one word—clingy.

Rajiv was also a victim of satellite love. He was both stubborn and short . . . stubborn because he kept at it despite a hundred rejections, and short . . . well, I don't have to explain how he was short, do I?

Classes were going on in full swing. After class, Rajiv would walk till the girls' hostel with Megha and would only head back when she had entered the building. One day, Rajiv stormed into our room and said to Dada, 'I want a gun!'

'Who are you gonna kill, bey?' Dada asked.

'You can see his dead body when I kill him!' Rajiv sputtered in rage.

'Tell us, bhai, what happened?' I asked.

'These fuckers are all jealous of me, they make jokes about me,' Rajiv said, wiping off beads of sweat.

'Again, you're confusing us! Are they jealous or are they making jokes? They're two different things,' Dada said.

'Dada! Let him speak, will you? Can't you see it's something serious?' I said.

'Abey, I haven't stuffed his mouth. He's the one who's not speaking, been sitting here tongue-tied.' Dada still wasn't being serious.

'Let me speak to him,' I interrupted.

'What happened, Rajiv?' I asked, putting my hand on his shoulder.

It was like Rajiv had been waiting for this small ounce of compassion. He broke down, and silently placed something resembling a crumpled piece of paper in front of me. It was not paper. It was a Dairy Milk chocolate wrapper.

Dada blew a fuse when he saw it.

'Motherfucker, you're crying for candy. Let's go to Lanka . . . we'll buy you some.'

'Dada, there's something written on it. Abey! This is a love letter!' I cried out, catching sight of some lettering.

'Read it out, let's see what's written there.' Dada sat up.

'I'll murder those assholes, I swear,' Rajiv flared up again.

'Shut up, you! Did nobody tell you that the content of a letter and the order of a waiter are the two things that should never be interrupted!' Dada thundered.

I started reading. The letter went like this:

Har Har Mahadev!
My Sorcerer,

Maybe it's the way you move, but you've got me dreaming like a fool, and I can feel your heartbeat running through me. You may ask me what's love got to do with it, but have I told you lately that I love you? Have I told you there's no one else above you? Even I have realized now that I ended up falling, falling, falling for you. You merely asked me, how would you feel if I told you I love you? But from that day on I was a believer. I'm never gonna give you up, never gonna run around and desert you, never gonna make you cry, so don't let me down, because

You are my love, you are my heart,
And we will never, ever, ever be apart.

Yours,
Shilpa Shetty

The moment I finished reading, the room erupted in laughter. Dada, who was nearly rolling on the floor, said, 'Bro! This looks like Shah Rukh Khan's letter. Where did you get it from?'

Rajiv was neither in the state nor in the mood to laugh. He was just about to snatch the wrapper from my hand and leave the room when Navenduji entered. He could tell by our looks that something interesting was up.

'All okay, Rajivji?' he asked.

Rajiv did not reply and just sat down on the bed silently.

'Shilpa Shetty's written a letter to Shah Rukh Khan and it's making Rajiv upset.' I was trying to control my laughter.

'Where is this letter?' Navenduji asked gravely.

Rajiv handed the wrapper again, this time to Navenduji. He looked even more grave after reading the letter and then said, 'This Shilpa Shetty seems to be playing games, huh? She's going around with Akshay Kumar and writing letters to Shah Rukh!'

This much was enough for room number 79 to explode into laughter once more. This time Rajiv did leave the room, cursing us all the way.

'If you want a story, a falsehood or a lie to spread in Bhagwandas, just mention it during meal-time at the mess. The job will be done. Rumours will do their work well and every molehill will become a mountain,' Navenduji said, waxing poetic.

'What's the story, Navenduji?' I was still trying not to laugh.

'So, Rajiv thinks Megha looks like Shilpa Shetty, and one time he said this in the mess. Today, when the two were returning from class, he gave Megha this chocolate. She refused at first, but when Rajiv insisted, she took it. She ate the chocolate and threw the wrapper away. Someone picked it up, wrote this love letter and slipped it inside Rajiv's room. You already know what happened next,' explained Navenduji in one long breath.

But what he had hidden was the culprit behind this incident. He was clever but not cunning, and certainly not more so than Dada. Before Dada could ask, however, I posed the question, 'So, Navenduji, who's the one who sowed charas in Rajiv's Eden of love?'

'I don't know, yaar!' Navenduji said, becoming shifty.

'You told us the whole story and now you say you don't know who the protagonist is! Will you tell us quickly or should we just declare it was you?' Dada threatened.

'Arre yaar, why do you keep tripping me up every opportunity you get? It's impossible to even tell you guys anything!' Navenduji was getting caught in his web of words now.

'Navenduji, if we talk about this outside, everyone will ask us who told us. Then we'll have no option but to name you. It's better you tell us here than people asking you outside, isn't it?' I said.

'Won't you guys ever listen?' Navenduji said.

'Nope,' Dada rejected him promptly.

'Man, Roshan is the one who told me. I don't know how he got to know.'

We weren't able to find out who had done this, but what we did find out the very next morning was that Rajiv had left the hostel and gone to live elsewhere.

Pyaar Koi Khel Nahi: Love Is Not a Game

Missing the first class on Monday was something of a rule. A late Sunday night out at Lanka was a weekly tradition. This was also called 'Lanketing' in the BHU dictionary. Lanka was the Connaught Place of BHU. After a night of Lanketing, someone or the other invariably missed the 10 a.m. class, but the good part was that one of the three of us would be there to give proxy attendance. Today was Dada's turn to sleep in. The one who came late went directly to the canteen and we met him there after class. So today, Dada was sitting in the canteen.

'What's up, bhai? Did M.P. Singh crack a joke? You can't stop laughing,' Dada asked, putting his legs up on the canteen bench.

'Guru, the drama happened before that,' Jaivardhan coughed.

'What happened? And why are you carrying around a long face?' Dada asked me.

'Ask me, I'll tell you! Here's what happened. This gentleman here missed breakfast, so he was entering the faculty eating a cream roll. He was late for class and M.P. Singh had already entered the classroom. The janitor had just wiped the floor. He slipped so hard that the cream roll went inside his mouth and his legs inside Section B, opposite the class he was supposed to be in.' Jaivardhan was laughing and coughing all at once.

'Oh no. You didn't get hurt, right? Two plates of samosa and three cups of tea!' Dada asked as he placed the order.

'Keep listening! The story isn't over yet. Now, our man had just slipped when a girl from Section B laughed. He's not as upset about falling as he is about the girl laughing.' Jaivardhan was still coughing and laughing at the same time.

'Who was it, man?' Dada asked.

'You can't expect me to give you her name and address. But she lives in room number 7 of Ganga Hostel,' I said softly.

'That's what I find so funny. He doesn't know her name but he's found out her correspondence address. And do you know from where? From Dubey, can you imagine? When the student is stupid but the teacher is stupider, one asks for a sweet and the other gives a stone.' Jaivardhan's laughter showed no signs of stopping.

'Never mind, kid. You didn't get hurt, right? Eat your samosas,' Dada said, eating one himself.

'I'm not upset about the fall, but when I fell the entire cream roll got stuffed into my face. Abey yaar, it was so embarrassing!' I explained as I picked up a samosa.

'The entire cream roll! A whole five inches! What a scene that must have been! I missed it, bro.' Dada was unable to hold back his laughter.

'That's why we tell you, you should attend classes once in a while,' Jaivardhan said as he stood up. Dada and I were just about to get up too when we saw someone entering the canteen.

'Look at that! It is her!' I said, looking at the canteen gate.

'The whole of Section B has come to the canteen. Which of these is it?' Dada asked.

'You see the one talking to Navenduji? Yes, her! Abey, what is she saying to Navenduji?' I asked softly.

'She's listening to Navenduji tell the story of *Veer–Zara*, that's what she's doing. Can't you shut up for a couple of minutes?' Dada said, annoyed.

'Look! Look! She laughed again and left! This is so embarrassing, yaar,' I told Jaivardhan.

'Let's go. We need to have a conversation with Navenduji,' Dada said, getting up from his chair.

'How are you doing, Navenduji?' Jaivardhan hollered from a distance.

'Everything is all right. I'm in a hurry right now, let's talk later.' Navenduji was suddenly itching to leave.

'No, wait! You seemed to be quite relaxed while talking to the young lady, and now that you see us, you're in a hurry?' Dada stopped him.

'What young lady?' Navenduji was getting uncomfortable.

'The same one you were talking to just a while ago!' Jaivardhan sneered.

'Oh, that . . . that's . . . Shikha. She was asking for Pande Sir's notes. Pande Sir doesn't teach in Section B, right, so that's why . . . ' Navenduji stuttered.

'You're the only student here, aren't you? Don't we study, huh?' Dada was not in the mood to accept Navenduji's clarifications.

'But I attend classes, at least. All of you should attend classes too. Pandeji was asking today if Anurag De is sick, he's come to class only four times in the whole month,' Navenduji said as he left the canteen.

'You effing duds. Did you mark my attendance only four days of the month? Motherfuckers . . . and I kept sleeping in the hostel because I trusted you.' Dada had changed gears now, turning his attention to us.

'And he didn't even mark all four. I proxied two of those times!' Jaivardhan said, adding fuel to the fire.

'Man, it's hard in Pandeji's class. He stays alert. I was about to do it today, then that girl laughed at me; it ruined my day.'

'To hell with that girl! Now I'll have to submit a medical certificate for attendance, and you're going to arrange that for me, got it?'

'I will, and don't worry bro, there's time. Professor will manage something. Come, let's go to Lanka, get some mango shake. Today is just not a good day. First, I fell down, then the girl laughed and now Navenduji walked off with an insult. But one good thing happened. At least

I found out her name, Shikha,' I said, climbing on to the pillion seat of the bike.

* * *

Assignments. In Jaivardhan's words, for people studying in the semester system, assignments were just like brides who couldn't stay long in their own homes but couldn't deal with their husbands' houses either. Assignments were worth a full twenty out of 100 so it wasn't possible to leave them, and for these twenty marks what we needed to spend was time—writing (or should we say copying) in the library, following professors around. There was one major expense for these assignments—accessories. Paper to write on, highlighters to decorate, plastic folders to present in, that kind of thing. We were going to get assignments too, but they were always accompanied by a series of idiotic events that were now underway in our room, the designated community hall.

'You people are worried about classes? Think about assignments—we need to submit ten assignments every semester. Tomorrow they'll start telling us the topics,' Dada said.

'What's there to worry about, we always have Google Baba to help!' I said.

'Yes, and our dean is Google Baba's boss! The instructions say that the project should be handwritten, not printed. Now you do the writing!' Dada said.

'I'm not doing any writing,' Jaivardhan replied flatly.

'Abey, it's worth twenty marks!' Dada said.

'Ghanta twenty marks,' Jaivardhan said, a bit annoyed.

'Okay, let's wait a little. Someone or the other will do it, right? Then that can be borrowed and copied. One night's worth of Dilip's tea, some cheap samosas and one project will be over. What do you say?' Dada suggested.

'Of course, asshole. And how will you write the project? Where's the paper?' I asked.

'It's there,' Dada said confidently.

'Vinod Varma bought an entire ream just yesterday. His room is right next to ours; he wakes up at 7 and goes to the bathroom. He usually takes an hour. Now, if in this time, his roommate's family calls and he goes down to talk, he won't lock the door, because Vinod will be in the washroom. That much time will be enough for the paper ream to shower its blessings on us,' Dada explained as he bit his nails.

Jaivardhan pointed out the issue: 'But how will his family call just then?'

'Why has Dhirubai given everyone 500-rupee phones, huh? We'll call the hostel's number from here and ask them to call Manish,' Dada said, waving his mobile in the air.

'And what if Vinod enters?' I asked, hoping to clear the final obstacle.

'He won't,' Dada said self-assuredly. When he goes to the bathroom he walks like Inzamam after another one of his run-outs. And, anyway, Jaivardhan will be there brushing his teeth at the nearby washbasin. He'll alert us if anybody approaches.'

'You freaking Bengali! You have an effing twisted head. All right, that's what we'll do. So, we've more or less arranged for the paper. Come, let's go buy some plastic folders and highlighters, or do you have a plan for those as well?' I laughed.

'No, motherfucker. Jugaad doesn't work everywhere, sometimes you have to use your hands as well.' Jaivardhan was also laughing.

'Come, let's go to Modern Pen Company, we'll buy all our stationery from there,' Dada said.

* * *

Modern Pen Company. If you went outside the BHU gate towards Heritage, then on the first floor was Modern Pen Company. All the stationery BHU students ever needed was available in this one shop, which is why the store was often crowded with students. But today there was nobody.

'What's up, Vipin, business is slow these days?' Dada asked the boy who worked at the store.

'Who do you think will come to the store in the afternoon?' Vipin replied.

'Okay . . . so give me two green highlighters, two rulers, and thirty plastic fol . . . '

I had not finished my sentence when a singsong voice interrupted me.

'Excuse me, do you have green highlighters?' said a girl who had just walked into the store with her friend.

'Abey, this is her! Shikha! The one from Section B!' I whispered in Dada's ear.

'Yes, I can see! God has blessed me with eyes too!' Dada was counting out the money.

Even the shopkeeper seemed more fond of her sweet voice than of my Banarasi tone, and he passed one of our highlighters to her. Dada saw this and was vexed.

'What have you given us one highlighter for? We asked for two, didn't we?'

'There are just two, so I gave you one and gave her one,' Vipin whimpered.

'Why, why did you pass it there, huh? Are we not paying you?'

Dada was engaging with him needlessly.

'Let it go, man,' I urged Dada.

'Let it go? Why should I let it go? We came and placed our order. We're paying and now he's saying he'll tie the match.' Dada was up for a fight, and I had to act the umpire.

'We'll manage with one, you may take it,' I said, passing the highlighter to Shikha.

'There's no need to create so much ruckus for one highlighter. Please give both to them,' Shikha said to the shopkeeper, ignoring me entirely.

'Ruckus, who's creating a ruckus? And what ruckus have you even seen so far, huh?' Dada said, furrowing his brows.

'Cool down, bro. Why are you getting hyper?' I asked Dada.

'Idiots,' we heard as Shikha stomped down the stairs with her friend.

'Hey . . . whom did you call an idiot?' Dada screamed behind her.

'Us, Dada. She called us I.D.I.O.T. I Do *Ishq* Only *Tumse*. I Love Only You. That's all she's said. You relax,' I said in an effort to lighten Dada's mood.

'Okay, but didn't she say idiots, not idiot?' Dada laughed.

'Yes, that's right, idiots. I Do Ishq Only Tumse, Suraj,' I said, giving Dada a high-five.

'And you, dumbass, you start speaking politely every time you see a girl, don't you? We'll manage with one, you may take it . . . that's what you said, huh?' Dada lit a cigarette the moment we got out.

* * *

Assignments were written till late into the night. This was because the people whose assignments we had to copy often completed them only by the evening. After intense persuasion, we would get their assignments at night. Tea to keep us awake all night was even more important than the assignments, and the tea was available at Lanka. Long nights at Lanka were thus spent drinking tea, eating buttered toast, discussing assignments and girls. We never realized how quickly time passed. When it was time for people to wake up at dawn, it was time for Dada and me to go to bed, and by the time we rose, the sun was invariably overhead.

'Where did my phone go?' Dada asked the minute he woke up.

'Jaivardhan's taken it; he's talking to someone outside,' I replied sleepily.

'Wake up, fucker, it's 10 already,' Dada said as he opened the windows.

'Just let me sleep, we wait so long for Sundays,' I said as I pulled the blanket over my face.

'Totally, you ass. You've blessed Bhagwandas by attending class every single day in the week, haven't you?' Dada opened the door as well.

'Bho . . . le . . . na . . . th . . . ' Dada shouted as he stretched.

'Listen, why don't you shout a little louder, so Bholenath shoots his *damru* to kill you, huh? Fricking disturbed my sleep with your shouting,' I said, covering my ears with a pillow.

'Wow, now people's sleep gets disturbed when you take the name of God!' Dada picked up his brush and toothpaste. When he reached the washbasin, he saw that Jaivardhan was pacing down the corridor, talking to someone on the phone. When Jaivardhan's conversation did not end even after he was done brushing, Dada could not hold himself back.

'Abey! Whom are you wasting my money on?' Dada shouted at Jaivardhan. 'Must be on with someone. Yesterday he was saying that if Sigmund Freud's written about it then there must be something special about women,' he murmured to himself.

'Even the last bill is unpaid, man, they'll cut my connection. Have some mercy,' Dada said, folding his hands before Jaivardhan.

'Here, take your phone and stick it up your ass. Oh, and put it on vibrate, you'll have more fun,' Jaivardhan said indignantly.

'Do phones come for free or what?' asked Dada.

'Dhirubhai Ambani's done it for 40 paise! Now are you expecting him to ask for scraps? If I've talked for ten minutes it's 4 rupees, the cost of one cigarette. If I talked for twenty, it's 8 rupees, the cost of two. You can smoke my cigarettes, all right,' Jaivardhan said.

'He's talked for full thirty-six minutes! Whom were you talking to, huh?' I asked as I looked at the phone.

'You know that boy from Patna, Abhishek? I was talking to him.' Jaivardhan could lay down his life for Patna.

'To a boy! Thirty-six minutes! Bhai, you haven't forgotten your chemistry, have you?'

'And when the two of you roam around all day on your bike like a lover and his loveress, which biology are you studying then?' Jaivardhan replied.

'But what were you saying to that Abhishek for half an hour?' I tried to lighten the mood.

'Oh, it's a really funny story. Let's go to the room, I'll tell you there.'

'Yes, what happened? What did you spend thirty-six minutes of your life on?' I asked as we entered the room.

'There was a presentation on contract in Section B yesterday,' Jaivardhan said.

'Oh, it's good that the presentation started in Section B. We'll get an idea of it,' I chimed in.

'Just shut up and listen, don't build walls when someone's waltzing!' Jaivardhan said crossly.

'So, when Abhishek was presenting, that girl Sonali, who hangs out with Shikha, clapped. Then what was to happen! Man, he forgot what he was saying. Ramji Sir said, never mind, go ahead, Abhishek, go ahead. Now Abhishek thought he meant "go forward", so he went a little ahead and stood next to Ramji Sir! The whole class laughed, but he only heard Sonali's laughter. He said it was like rose petals falling. He even quoted some poetry, something like this:

> When she must have looked at me with love
> She must have thought of me carefully enough.

He's saying he's in love, won't be able to live without her.'

Jaivardhan was thoroughly enjoying telling us this story.

'Who's this Sonali now?' Dada asked, lying on his bed as he bounced a tennis ball off the wall.

'Remember the other girl that day, with Shikha, at Modern Pen Company? That's Sonali,' I explained.

'You seem to know a lot about girls. Are you getting this news from Al Dubeira, huh?' Dada asked.

'Forget Dubeyji and his news for a second. Come on, listen to what happened next,' Jaivardhan said.

'Oh, your thirty-six minutes aren't up? Go on,' I said.

'Abhishek was saying he wants to talk to her, tell her how he feels, so he needs her phone number.'

'What does he need her phone number for? Tell him if he can't hold it in, he can call on the girls' hostel landline,' Dada said, throwing the tennis ball my way.

'He did. He was saying the girls' hostel landline is always busy and when he gets through, he has to tell them Sonali's room number to be able to get her on the phone. He doesn't know her room number or her phone number, so how will he talk to her?'

'And?' Dada asked.

'And I told him I'll arrange it,' Jaivardhan said.

'You? How will you arrange it? You're a dumbass, that's what you are,' Dada scolded.

'What could I have done? He hyped up my ego!' Jaivardhan said.

'And why do you keep falling for this ego hype?' I asked.

'What should I fall for then? Ghanta? He says let alone someone from outside, even a hosteller can't arrange someone's phone number from the girls' hostel. Even the devil has a soft spot for hell, and, plus, this is a matter of the hostel's honour,' Jaivardhan said.

'Is that so?' Dada asked.

'Of course, and if we get the number, he'll lose 1000 rupees.' Now, Jaivardhan had got to the useful part.

'1000 rupees!' I exclaimed, as my eyes widened.

'Yes, 1000 rupees!' Jaivardhan incited us.

'Then go, go ask if he'll give 500 rupees in advance,' Dada said, reading *Sports Star*.

'From whom are you taking 500 rupees as bribe, huh?' Vineet Singh said as he entered the room.

'Oh, come in, come in, Mr Minister. Been so long, where have you been? No news of you, you don't even come to class these days,' Dada greeted him.

'We are lovers, this is how we get by: we flit, we float, we fleetly flee, we fly,' Vineet said poetically, as he took out a pistol from inside his shirt and kept it on the table.

'Hey, Mr Minister! Don't bring weapons into the hostel, we'll get thrown out of here,' I said, covering the pistol with a towel.

'And don't keep its trigger upwards, bro. If it gets pressed accidentally someday, our necks will get blown off,' Dada added.

'And if we keep the trigger downwards the stuff will get blown off. We'll manage if our necks get blown off, but it'll be a problem if the other things are,' Vineet said with a laugh. 'Oh, what's for lunch in the mess today?'

'Who knows? Just been listening to ballads of love all morning,' I said.

'Whose ballads of love?' Vineet winced.

'Just one of these batchmates, lives in Chittupur. Wants the phone number of one of the girls from the girls' hostel,' Dada said.

'Whose number?' Vineet asked.

'There's this girl in Section B, Sonali,' I said.

'I think she's in Ganga Hostel, but I don't know her room number,' Jaivardhan piped up.

'When you go to the office this evening, you can take the number from me. Now come, let's get something to eat in the mess,' Vineet remarked casually.

* * *

Office. It was located right between Pratap Hotel and Banaras Burger Centre or, in other words, the place in front of Gopal Mango Shake. It was the place where the student ministers of Birla Hostel lived. Whether it was a test or a film preview, batting or flirting, cricket or kabaddi, the debates always started here at 4 p.m. and went on till 4 a.m. Politics was an evergreen topic. From major rows to minor skirmishes, every problem was solved here either with a mango shake or mini pistol class.

'Mr Minister, what are the new updates in the office?' I asked Vineet as soon as we reached.

'Just the same old: the demand for a student union. I did meet the vice chancellor today, and he said he'll forward the demand to the education ministry. Let's see, maybe something good will happen this time,' Vineet said as he sipped his mango shake.

'Why are you trying to breathe life into a corpse? The student union was dead way back. You guys are unnecessarily going door to door,' Dada said.

'No. The student union is in coma thanks to people like you. Yaar, if you can't help, don't, but at least don't insult us! Don't worry, we will bring it out of its coma.

Then you'll see what student power is! Until then we fight, my friend!' he said, quoting Pash's poetry.

'All right, you keep up your work, and tell me whether our job is done,' I said.

'Oh, was that even a job? Here, note it down,' he said and started dictating a number written on his hand.

'You got it really easily, guru! How did you arrange for it?' Dada asked.

'You see that boy on the Yamaha bike? The one in the green T-shirt?'

'Yes, yes, he's an IT student, name's Ankit. Even his girlfriend is in IT. Zooms around on his bike all day,' I said.

'Exactly. Even you're pretty updated, kid. Once I was asking everyone for bikes for the rally. When I went to the IT hostel, this was the only guy who didn't give his bike. Said he had to go to watch a film in the evening, *Munna Bhai MBBS*. What's more, when I met him at the office the next day and asked him why he was watching *MBBS* when he was studying IT, he started whimpering. Said he'd made a mistake and that he'd give me the bike anytime I asked for it. And would even fill in the petrol,' Vineet said, fiddling with the ring on his finger.

'That's some good stuff! But how did you get the number?' I asked.

'Bro, his girlfriend is as cunning as he is simple. Lives in Ganga Hostel. She's arranged two to three numbers before too. Now, for example, she wanted Sonali's number, so she went to her room. Made some small talk, got to know her a little. Then, while leaving, she left her phone there on purpose. She went back a while later, upset, and told Sonali she'd left her phone somewhere, so could Sonali call it. As soon as it rang, she said, 'Look! How stupid I am, looking for my phone everywhere after leaving it here.' That's how she got Sonali's number without her suspecting a thing!' Vineet narrated.

'Wow, that's one explosive woman! Whichever house she gets married into is sure to become heaven! She really is cunning!' Dada said.

'But bhai, why did you write the number on your hand? You could have saved it on your phone,' I said.

'No, man! It's a girl's number, it'll be a problem if I forget to delete it. You know my phone's like a booth, everyone uses it. It's just because Jaivardhan had placed a bet and it was a question of the hostel's honour that I arranged for it. Now you figure out what to do with it. Just remember, every woman is someone's sister,' Vineet explained.

'Of course, Mr Minister! We'll just give Jaivardhan the number and take 1000 rupees,' Dada said.

'Okay, I'll go now; there's a procession in Durgakund. I'll get late,' Vineet said, starting his Bullet.

'Wow, man! A cheque for 1000 rupees!' I said to Dada.

'First check whether the number's correct or Mr Minister just got the better of us!'

'Yes, come, let's call,' I said, dialling the number.

'Listen, you dumbass, don't use your phone. The number will show up on her phone, and what if she gives it to the proctor?' Dada said, freaking out a little.

'Yes, man! You're right. Let's dial it from the telephone booth.'

'Did it connect?' Dada asked, pressing his ear to the phone.

'It's ringing . . . it's ringing!'

'Hey, why did you hang up now?'

'Abey, a girl picked up!' I was nearly trembling.

'Which means Minister gave us the correct number,' Dada said.

'Let's go now, let's get our 1000 rupees from Jaivardhan.'

* * *

After returning from Lanka that evening, Dada gave Jaivardhan the number and explained that arranging 1000 rupees was now his duty. Jaivardhan was taking a shower when we left for tea the next morning. He had taken Dada's phone to call someone at home. We were just leaving after telling him to meet us at the tea shop when we caught sight of Dubeyji, standing on the hostel terrace.

'Dubeyji! Why are you standing on Bhagwandas's head?' I shouted out to him.

'Can't you see, I'm on a call!' Dubeyji said, gesturing towards the phone.

'Fucker! Got us all to eat rotten food at the mess and now he's bought a phone! Just look at him!' Dada said, craning his neck.

'You look at him and look carefully. That's your phone,' I told him.

'What! My phone!' Dada was close to tears.

'Jaivardhan must have given it to him; the two seem to be bonding these days.'

'This time when the bill comes . . . I'll have to throw my phone away into the Ganga.' Dada was holding his head.

'Come, let's get some tea, we'll figure this out when we return,' I assured him.

'Wait, let me get a cigarette first. Dubey has spoiled my mood.'

'Avdhesh, make some tea and two plates of omelette-samosa,' I told the man at the teashop.

'Make that three plates. Look, Jaivardhan is also coming,' Dada said. Dada felt relieved to see the phone in Jaivardhan's hand. The way Jaivardhan was laughing as he entered made it clear that something was definitely up.

'What happened? Be careful, fucker, don't fall over. What are you laughing so much for?' Dada said, looking at Jaivardhan.

'It's so funny, even you'll go crazy laughing if you hear.'

'What happened, did you see something you shouldn't have?' I joked.

'No, but there's something I'm about to see—your funeral pyre,' Jaivardhan laughed, looking at me.

'Will you tell us what happened?' Dada asked.

'I will but get Baba out of the way first. His heart will fail if he hears,' Jaivardhan said.

'My heart is in pieces anyway, strewn all over the girls' hostel. Anyway, you go on,' I said somewhat poetically.

'Okay, then listen. Dubey called Sonali, said some nonsense to her. She disconnected two to three times, but when he called repeatedly, she retorted with something that made him cut the call,' Jaivardhan said, keeping his laughter in check.

'What did she say?'

'Said "You're Suraj speaking, aren't you?" That was it, and then Dubey cut the call.' Jaivardhan controlled himself for a bit and then started laughing again.

'What!' I sputtered.

'Here you go! Now you're done for. Go, look for a room in Chittupur, the hostel's out of your hands now.' Dada was also laughing his head off now.

'But fucker, why did he cut the call? Now she probably thinks I'm definitely the one who called!' I said, dejected.

'Don't get too worried, Dubey has fixed everything,' Jaivardhan said, suppressing a giggle.

'Thank god. How did he fixed it?' I asked, heaving a sigh of relief.

'Dubey called again and said, "I'm not Suraj." Then he disconnected the call.' Jaivardhan burst into laughter again.

'What? Oh my god! Is this Dubey a man or a donkey! Now she must be completely sure that it was I who called. Why did he have to call again?' I said, holding my head in my hands.

Jaivardhan and Dada were laughing uncontrollably, and this was making me angrier.

'And all of you who're giggling right now! When you get stuck, I'm going to be the one to get you out!' I said irritatedly.

'First get yourself out, man. Go, go to the proctor's office. And listen, don't forget to wear a tie. I've heard that guy Tiwari, from the proctor's office, is looking for a groom for his wife. You'll make a good impression,' laughed Dada.

'But where did Dubey get the number from?' I asked suddenly.

'I had tried the number yesterday, so it was the first in the call details. God knows what came over Dubey . . . he dialled it!' Jaivardhan said.

'Which means I've been in trouble since last night! I'll have to do some talking.'

'Just listen to me, you don't have to say anything to anyone. You haven't done anything at all,' Dada said.

'Bro, she must be thinking I make prank calls!'

'Then let her think. That's her problem, not yours.' Dada lit a cigarette again.

'Even then, I feel like I should clear the confusion. I'll speak to Shikha,' I said.

'Why would you speak to Shikha? Talk directly to Sonali, no?' Jaivardhan said.

'No, talking to her directly can mess up the situation. Shikha is her roommate; she can explain it to her,' I said, throwing away the *kulhad* I was drinking from.

'Baba, just say directly that you're looking for an excuse to talk to Shikha,' Dada said.

'Whatever. I have to do some talking.'

* * *

Actually, Dada was right. I had been trying to talk to
Shikha for a long time. First, she was in a different section,
and second, no opportunity had presented itself. Either
she was surrounded by her friends or mine were always
with me. Plus, the Modern Pen Company incident had
dampened my spirits. It was quite possible she didn't want
to talk to me after that, so I thought it would be a good idea
to speak to her when she was alone. I got this opportunity
during an exam. Shikha had submitted her answer sheet a
little early, and I was strolling outside having submitted my
sheet already, when I saw her.

'Shikha!' I said, coming outside the faculty gate.

'Yes?' came her singsong voice.

'Hello, I'm Suraj,' I started to introduce myself.

'Yes, I know. I saw you that day at Modern Pen
Company,' she replied slowly.

'How was the paper?' There could not be a better excuse
than this to start a conversation.

'It was good. And yours?' she asked.

'Not so good. The carbolic smoke ball case took up too
much time, so I couldn't complete one of the questions.'

'Really? But they didn't ask anything from offer and
acceptance, right?' Shikha said thoughtfully.

'No, no, I wrote it in the question about formation and
contract,' I replied hurriedly. Now, I couldn't tell her that
according to Dubey's Formula One, you only wrote what
you remembered, irrespective of what the question was.

'Hmm . . . maybe.' She was still thinking about
something.

'And listen, there's one more thing,' I hesitated.

'Yes, go on,' Shikha said, adjusting her bag.

'You have a classmate, right? Sonali? She thinks I prank call her!'

'Yes, she does get some prank calls.' Shikha looked at me suspiciously.

'But I didn't make those calls,' I replied quickly.

'Just a minute. If you didn't make the calls, then how did Sonali receive them?' Shikha said suddenly. I had got trapped in my own words.

'I found out from my friends,' I said, trying to handle the situation somehow.

'She didn't tell anyone. I know because she's my roommate. Which means that either it's you making the calls or those so-called friends of yours in the hostel.' Shikha had caught me again.

'Man, it's not fair to drag the hostel into the picture every time. It's nobody from the hostel. I do know the one who made the call, but he's not from the hostel. I don't want any misunderstanding.'

'Don't worry, you are no Tom Cruise, so there won't be a misunderstanding. I'll tell Sonali what you said, though.'

'Thanks.'

'Tell me something. You could have said this to Sonali too, then why me?' Shikha asked suddenly again.

'So, there are no misunderstandings.'

'Misunderstanding. With whom?' Shikha sounded upset.

'With you.'

'With me? Why would there be any misunderstanding with me?' She was getting annoyed now.

'Because I love you.' I did not embellish my words.

'What?!' She was not prepared for this.

'Yes.' I was prepared.

'Excuse me! Do I know you?' she said.

'You just said a while ago that you knew me. Look, don't go back on your word now.'

'Do you want to get married?'

'What?!' I was not prepared for this.

'I know you rascals very well. First, you prank people all night, then you put on a facade of decency. Get going now or the dean's chamber is just here on the right.' She was prepared for this.

* * *

Assi Ghat. The first ghat when you go northwards, where the Varuna and Assi rivers meet. The ghat of saints, the ghat of swindlers. The ghat of poets, the ghat of pictures. The smokers' ghat, the drinkers' ghat. My ghat. Dada's ghat. Our ghat.

'Bhaiya, two cups of tea!' Dada said as soon as he sat down.

'Ask for some snacks too.'

'To hell with snacks! Do you think my father has a treasury? Anyway, what is the conversation you were having at the faculty gate yesterday?'

'How do you know?' I asked, throwing rocks into the Ganga.

'A millipede at the faculty gate often becomes a cobra by the time it reaches the hostel, Baba! Anyway, what did you talk about yesterday?' Dada picked up two teacups.

'Tell me, Dada, have you ever proposed to a girl?' I asked, taking one from him.

'Once in BCom, I said I love you to her.'

'And?'

'And the girl said okay. Damn! I still haven't understood how "okay" can be a response to "I love you". Yes, no, honey, idiot, donkey, asshole—she could have said anything; she could have shown me my face in the mirror or shown me the slippers on my feet, but why say okay?' Dada said, sipping his tea.

'Now don't make me laugh! I'll die.' I had started to snort tea from my nose.

'Yes, you idiot, you laugh. Now that you're in trouble, I'll laugh! All of Bhagwandas will laugh!' Dada said, tossing away his cup.

'Okay, let's go back to the hostel now. I don't feel like being here anymore,' I said.

'Wait, my friend! Now you'll feel like being here. Look there, look who's come in the boat.' It was Shikha.

'Oh, my! All the way to Ganga Vihar by boat, and that too without me! You go to the hostel, I will come in a bit,' I told Dada and started going down the steps.

'It's happened, hasn't it? The girl has come between friends, hasn't she? You used to say a lot about friendship.

Fucker, you drank about seventy glasses of mango shake and now you're leaving! All right then, this friendship is over. We spend our own money from now on.' Dada's voice followed me till I reached the boat.

'Hello,' I said, stopping near the boat.

'You? What are you doing here?' Shikha asked.

'Now I'm a rascal, I can go anywhere I want. As of now, I'm looking for Tulsidas at the ghat, have to get him some pizza,' I laughed.

'I am not amused,' Shikha smirked.

'Listen, there's a famous restaurant here, The Pizzeria. The mushroom pizza there is pretty good,' I said.

'Thanks for the information,' she replied disinterestedly.

'Can we sit there for ten minutes?' I begged.

'Why?' she asked, paying the boatman.

'Because I've just pickpocketed someone and us rascals have a rule. We spend the money where we get it from. I am not able to spend it, so I'm requesting you.'

'Will you not listen?' she glared at me.

'Why don't you listen this one time?' I requested again.

'All right, come, but only ten minutes. I have to go to the hostel as well.'

'If they prepare the pizza in ten minutes and you eat it as well, I certainly don't mind.'

The Pizzeria—the pizza joint built on the upper side of Assi Ghat. The meeting point of foreign tourists. You could order one pizza and enjoy the waves of the Ganga for the entire evening, but I didn't have the entire evening, a mere ten minutes. I didn't want to waste even a single second. As soon as we reached The Pizzeria, I sat at a table and picked up a menu card.

'You order.' I handed the menu card to Shikha.

'All right, at least you know that much. Two mushroom pizzas, is that okay?'

'Yes,' I agreed and then said, 'So you think I'm a good-for-nothing rascal!'

'What do you do? You don't study, that's for sure. Your classes run in the canteen. Even in the combined classes, I've only seen you proxying for people. So, what is it that you do?'

'I explore poetry, I weave dreams,' I said, looking into her eyes.

'Then you should have been in the arts faculty. Why are you here?' she said promptly.

'You weren't there in the arts faculty else I would have taken history, civics, geography, anything.' I did not take my eyes off hers.

'You talk pretty smoothly, is your poetry like this as well? Recite something.'

'What will I get if I recite something?' I took a chance.

'Are you in a position to make deals?' she glared.

'Yaar, this is not fair. Artists should be respected, at least in Banaras,' I said, picking up a slice.

'Okay, if I like it, the next treat is on me, but I have to like it,' she said, sprinkling chilli flakes on her pizza.

'Okay. There will be a few complex words.' I finished the second slice and started reciting.

I hear people all watch her, transfixed
So let me stay awhile in her city and take a look.

I hear she is drawn to the damaged, the most broken souls
So let me break all that I am and take a look.

I hear when she speaks there is a shower of flowers
And even the fireflies all pause, just to take a look.

I hear her tresses are darker than the darkest nights
And when the shadows pass at dusk, even they take a look.

I hear even the roses are envious of her lips
Now let me put the blame on spring so I can take a look.

I hear that the art of her body is such
That the flowers snip their petals just to take a look.

I finished the poem and looked at Shikha. She was listening keenly.

'Hmm. Nice. Is it yours?' she asked, cupping her face in her hands.

'No, it's for you,' I smiled.

'You could be a good lawyer. You give good arguments.' She wiped the corners of her lips with a tissue.

'You can't be a good judge. You never give answers,' I said, paying the bill.

'All right, the next treat is on me. You decide the date, I'll decide the venue.'

'You dodged my question again.'

'You boys are such idiots. Didn't you notice that I've been sitting here for half an hour? Bye. Take care,' Shikha said, smiling mysteriously. 'Oh, and by the way, it's civics in school, it's political science in college. Do a little studying sometimes too,' she said softly and quickly walked out of the restaurant.

I kept searching for the meaning of her smile after I paid the bill. She said that she sat for half an hour after saying ten minutes at first, which meant she also liked being with me. Why did she insist on hearing a poem? But when did she insist? Can a girl just eat pizza like this with a boy? Why did she talk about another treat? Did she also want to meet me? Did she also like me? Or . . . or . . . or was I becoming a victim of satellite love?

* * *

I was in the pizzeria even after returning to the hostel. I didn't feel like being in the room, so I took my discman to the hostel terrace. I did run the risk of being shouted at by those in Gurtu Hostel opposite ours, but I wanted to be alone—to look for answers to the questions that were bothering me. Was Shikha also feeling like this? Was she also strolling on her hostel terrace? There would be no fear of being shouted at on her terrace. All that chaos was limited to ours. But if you put on your earphones, you won't hear anyone, I thought.

'What are you listening to sitting alone on the terrace?' Jaivardhan asked as he came in.

'Come, sit,' I told him as I saw him approach.

However, I could not hear what he said.

'Go on, what is it that you're listening to, all alone?' Jaivardhan asked, taking the earphones out of my ear.

'Munni Begum.'

'Oh, courtesan music!' Jaivardhan put the earphone on for a moment and then took it out.

'Munni Begum doesn't sing courtesan music, she sings ghazals,' I retorted.

'It's all the same, guru! You enjoy it, right? That's all you need! You should enjoy it. That's what matters,' Jaivardhan said philosophically.

'It really is useless to talk to you,' I said, switching off the discman.

'Let's go then, let's go Lanketing. Otherwise come downstairs. It's about to get dark. The guys in Gurtu will start cursing us now,' said Jaivardhan, getting up.

'Sit down, man, I don't feel like going out today,' I said, pulling Jaivardhan down by his hand.

'Guru, what's up with you?' Jaivardhan checked my forehead for fever.

'Man, I think I "be" falling in love,' I replied in Murali's Sir's style.

'We are not being those people. Friendship is okay, but we can't be lovers. You will be having to change your thoughts,' Jaivardhan joked.

'Come on, don't joke!' I scolded.

'I thought you were joking, Baba! Is it Shikha?'

'Yes.'

'Arre haan, I totally forgot to ask! What happened that day?' Jaivardhan had settled down comfortably by then.

'I looked at her and I kept looking. What else do I say, and what else is there to say?' I said with the air of a romantic poet as I stared at the sky.

'Come on, fucker! A kid goes off to a Mughal country and returns knowing just the Mughal tongue. He dies of thirst since when he asked for water no one understood, though it was right there all along.'

'What does this mean?' I asked, surprised.

'Did I ask you the meaning of your poem? Fricking politely asked you what happened and you started throwing poetry at me!'

'I don't remember what happened. I just remember her eyes; everything else is gone!'

'What? You must remember something!'

'Yes, I proposed to her.'

'Jiyo Raja Banaras! And the response from the other party?'

'What do you think? Why do you think I sit here on the terrace listening to Munni Begum every day? That's the problem, there was no response,' I replied sadly.

'You mean the rabbi waits while the bride escapes?' Jaivardhan came out with another idiom.

'Yes, something like that.'

'Then keep meeting her, give it some time. Something or the other will come out of it.'

'I've met her three to four times. I've just returned from meeting her.'

'Oh . . . the telecast is already on. This is what Roshan was talking about, then.'

'What was he saying?'

'He was asking, is Suraj serious?'

'And what did you say?'

'I said he's very serious. His bilirubin is at 13.50. He's going to kick the bucket this time and maybe you should too,' Jaivardhan laughed.

The evening was turning into night. The electricity had also gone out. It was a good idea to head downstairs. The dissemination of expletives would also start soon. This was a tradition that had been carried out for decades between the two hostels when the lights went out. Since the boys had nothing else to do, this was the normal method of entertainment. We were just about to head downstairs when a voice called, 'Hey, oldies of Bhagwandas! How much longer are you going to study?'

This had come from Gurtu Hostel. The onslaught of abuses was about to begin.

'You're messing around with your boss, huh? Is this what your mother has taught you?' Jaivardhan shouted in reply.

'Yes, Papa! Mumma was asking how much longer you're going to study! Do some actual work now!'

'Amit, my son, it's because of some actual work that you came to be. Anyway, since you're asking, I'll go. I'll give your mother a dose again,' Jaivardhan said as we started climbing down.

'Who's this Amit? Do you know him?' I asked.

'Who knows! It's such a common name, there must be someone or the other called that. You throw a pebble into a crowd, it's bound to hit an Amit or a Santosh or a Rahul. Wait now, everything will go silent.'

'Bro, your trick actually worked! Everyone actually went silent. But man, what's Roshan's problem?' I asked myself.

* * *

Maybe it was just because of the projects and presentations, but I had started talking to Shikha now. Now we didn't have to flatter anybody, at least for assignments. Shikha would submit a project in Section B, and the three of us would submit the same project in Section A. So, her arrival was like a dream come true for us. Often, I would leave my friends and sit with Shikha in the canteen and both my friends would not get offended at this. After all, it was a question of projects and assignments. There was one thing though: Shikha refused to speak to Dada after the Modern Pen Company incident and so she had never spoken to Jaivardhan either. But she never opposed my friendship with them. She would often get annoyed by the Modern Pen Company incident, so I avoided mentioning it.

Today was a combined class and, unfortunately, not one of us three was present. All of us were standing outside.

'The class is over. Shrivastav Sir is going to take attendance. As soon as he reaches roll number 10, we have to tiptoe in quietly,' I said, peering into the classroom from a corner of the door.

'Listen, you enter alone and proxy for all three of us,' Dada suggested.

'Sure, motherfucker! I had introduced myself as Anurag during the last class. He's already started doubting me.'

'Look, the attendance has begun. It's a combined class, even Shikha is in there! There are a lot of students, he won't suspect anything. Go in quickly.' Dada pushed me inside. I somehow sat on the last bench and started paying attention to the attendance.

'Roll number 27.'

'Yes, sir,' I said.

'Roll number 29'

'Present, Sir,' I said, a little hurriedly.

'Your name?' Shrivastav Sir looked up.

'Jaivardhan Sharma.'

'Father's name?' Shrivastav Sir had started to suspect me.

'Sorry?'

'You must know your father's name, right? Or did you think you would never need it?' Sir smiled. The whole class started to laugh as I just stood there.

'What is your name?'

'Suraj,' I replied, looking at the floor.

'Yesterday you said you were Anurag! Jaivardhan, Anurag and you are to meet me in my chamber after class.'

'Okay, Sir. But please mark me present today,' I requested.

'Roll number 30,' Shrivastav Sir moved on without answering me.

Class was over. I had been disgraced, that too in a combined class. Shikha kept sitting even after the entire class had left. I realized it was not about explaining things anymore, so I moved slowly towards her. She started to get up from her seat when she heard me approaching.

'Listen. I'm sorry.' I surrendered.

'If you don't want to attend class, don't. But why do you have to accept the contract for the attendance of the whole class?' Shikha snapped.

'Man, those people proxy for me too.'

'That's great. That means favours are being returned here, that's great. Do me a favour too. Don't proxy, at least in combined classes.' Shikha was quite annoyed today.

'I'm sorry. Just let it go. Want to have some tea?' I said to calm her down.

'Thanks. But please, leave me alone,' she said and started walking towards the canteen alone. I was the only one left in the classroom. Before I could think of anything, Dada and Jaivardhan entered from the back door.

'Idiot, don't you know how to proxy for someone? Got us in trouble, didn't you?' Dada said.

'Don't fuck with my head right now. I'm not in a good mood.'

'You idiot, nothing happened in the past three classes when I proxied for you. Courage, that's what you need,' Jaivardhan said.

'So what? I was helping you guys out! The whole day went by with Dubey. Thank god for him, he knows a doctor, he's arranged for a medical certificate. Now you'll be able to appear for the exam,' I said in a single breath.

'Bholenath! You are Raja Hindustani, my friend!' Dada shouted loudly.

'Let's go to Vishwanath Mandir, I'll buy you some shake,' Jaivardhan said as we walked out.

'No, you go, I'm going to Lanka for a bit. She's in a bad mood. I'll have to give her some time,' I said.

'Okay, okay, go on, Baba. Go fix her mood. We have five projects left. We've copied all the other five from her anyway. You go, give her my thanks, and don't worry about Shrivastav Sir. If he's the boss, so am I. We'll figure something out.' Dada laughed, got on the bike with Jaivardhan and left.

* * *

7 p.m. The same day.

'What happened, Baba? Why is your shirt torn? And where did this wound come from? Were you in an accident?' Dada asked, opening the door.

'No, man. I've been in a fight, not an accident.' I put a bottle of water to my lips.

'You mean someone hit you? Motherfucker! Who had the courage . . . Jaivardhan! Jaivardhan!' Dada called out.

'I don't know. I don't know them. I was returning after meeting Shikha. She found a friend, so left early. I was on my way back when a few boys showed up.'

'Come, let's go right now. It's time to go see who's in the mood to play with fire today. Where has this Jaivardhan gone?' Dada said in a fit of rage.

'How will going there help? It's not like you're going to find someone there. Come, sit. I'm fine and don't call Jaivardhan here. He'll hand anyone the blame just by the way they look.'

'But you don't even have any issues with people. What problem would anyone have with you?'

'Someone certainly does!'

'What do you mean?' Dada sat up.

'I mean I was threatened to stay away from Shikha. Told that she's from a good family.'

'And it's not like you're Don's only son!'

'There's one more thing.'

'What?'

'One of them snatched my wallet but did not take any money. He just took my ID card and fled.'

'What else could he have done? It's not like your wallet had any money. I checked your wallet today, there wasn't even a rupee in it.'

'There was. I met Uncle on the way to Lanka.'

'Which uncle? Since when do you have an uncle in Banaras?'

'Your father, Mr De. He gave me 2000 rupees and asked me to give it to you. For your mess fees.'

'Then give me the money!' Dada held out his hand.

'I told you, there was money. Now it's gone. We went to Lanka Cafe, it got spent there,' I laughed.

'You fucking idiot! Asshole. Motherfucker ate away my mess money, I'm glad they gave you a beating, very well done,' Dada fumed.

'Here, there's some money left, keep it. I didn't tip them so it got saved.' I tried to suppress my laughter.

'How much more nonsense will you spout?' Dada was also laughing now. Just then, the phone began to ring.

'Look, the phone's ringing. Check who's calling,' I told Dada.

'I don't know who's calling! You see for yourself!' Dada said angrily.

'Oh, it's Shikha! Hello?' I said, taking the call.

'Did you have a fight with someone today?' she got straight to the point.

'Who told you?' I asked furtively.

'A question is not meant to be answered with a question.'

'No, man. It was just a simple argument.'

'You didn't get hurt, did you?'

'No. I just lost my ID card,' I said, hiding the truth.

'Oh! Then complain to the police!'

'A police complaint just for one ID card! Won't that be a bit much?'

'I'm saying it for your own good. You're studying law, at least use your grey matter a little.'

'All right, I'll do it tomorrow morning. And, what's up?' I tried to change the topic.

'Goodnight,' she said and hung up.

'She hung up, man! Gave so much lecture and when it was time to talk, she just said goodnight!' I said, disappointed.

'What lectures were you listening to?' Dada asked.

'Just that I should report my missing ID card.'

'So, will you go to the station tomorrow?'

'No, man! There are too many things in this world more important than an ID card,' I said and went straight to sleep.

Mandi: The Market

The third-semester exams were over. The Criminal Procedure Code (CrPC) paper was exactly the same as the one we had got, so that one was the easiest to score in. The other papers were also okay. Dada and Jaivardhan's exams went better than mine. They were sure they wanted to make a career in law, but I hadn't been able to decide what I wanted to do yet. Even though Shikha met me every day and told me to get serious about my career, I did not want to go into law at all. As of now, I was just living by the day. This day, in Banaras. This day, with Shikha. This day, in my hostel. And this day, with my friends.

'Don't eat so much bread-pakora; jaundice can relapse also,' Dada said, snatching the snack from my hand.

'The bilirubin's all right, man. I eat it only after dabbing it with paper.'

'Abey, do you squeeze out the bread's oil or the paper's oil? Look! There's oil on Sania Mirza's photo. Damn, you can't make anything out! Now I'll have to go to Balkishun's shop to get a good look at Sania!' Jaivardhan said, squinting.

'So read it in the hostel,' I offered him a solution.

'You know what I'll get in the hostel? Ghanta! The others must have already taken it to their rooms and cut out the photo and pasted it,' Jaivardhan said as he sipped his tea.

'Have you seen Alankar's room? He's turned it into a barber's shop! Abey, give me the bread na!' I said as I tried to grab it.

'Alankar's very fond of cars. He's put up photos of every model from an Audi to a Hummer,' Dada said.

'What strange people we have here!' Jaivardhan said, peering at Sania Mirza's photo.

Dhola teri kamaal aaye,
Nikki ji gal tu rushde
Dhola teri kamaal aaye.

I broke into song, giving beats to it on Jaivardhan's back.

'Will you sing one song in Hindi before I die? Whom do you sing these Hebrew songs for in Banaras?' Dada said, throwing away his kulhad.

'Come on! Martab Ali's new album has just released in Pakistan!'

'Yes, and Sunil Singh will make you perform antics, here in Hindustan,' Jaivardhan said.

'Abey, who's this Sunil Singh?' I asked.

'The villain for third-year students. The demon of room number 100. He called me to his room yesterday and said, "Tell that boy you hang out with to shut up when he's goes to the bathroom from tomorrow, or I'll stuff his goddamn mouth with bamboo. Keeps croaking like a broken flute every morning, spoils both my day and my sleep'.' Jaivardhan said, slapping Dada's shoulder.

'Did you sing in a train earlier, Baba?' Dada teased.

'Broken flute! My girlfriend used to tell me I sing like Kishore Kumar.' I was really upset.

'Was she a busker on a train earlier, huh?' It was now Jaivardhan's turn. Even as the two stopped laughing, someone called out from behind.

'Anurag Bhaiya.'

The man seemed to be a labourer. His pants were covered in mud, his face hidden by a beard, unshaven for about a week. His body was covered in sweat. It was clear that he was unhappy about something.

'What's wrong?' Dada asked.

'Are you Bengali?' It was a strange question.

'No, he's Bangladeshi. His grandfather escaped from Bangladesh without a ticket and was stopped at Mughalsarai. The TTE made him get off the train, so he settled down there.' I made the most of the chance.

'Go fuck yourself, man! Can't you shut up for a couple of minutes?' Nothing angered Dada like being called a Bangladeshi.

'What's the matter?' Dada asked the man.

The man held out a sheet of paper and said, 'Please read what's written here. I'm illiterate. I work in concrete casting in Chittupur. Someone told me that the writing is in Bengali and someone here can read it.'

'But who told you about me?' asked Dada, taking the paper in his hands.

'When I showed the paper at a teashop in Chittupur, someone told me there's one "Anurag Bangali" in Bhagwan Hostel. I asked around till I found the place.'

'*Lo beta*! You've become a star now! People know you even in Chittupur. Anurag Bangali. Like there's Baba Akram Shah Bangali, there's also Anurag Bangali! Do you practise hypnosis, Dada? Do you also fix cases of unrequited love?' I teased.

'Where did you find this paper?' Dada asked, ignoring me.

The man got a little shifty at this question. After a few moments of silence, he said: 'Well, there's no reason to hide it from you! I had gone to Manduadih yesterday, met a girl there. She started crying as soon as we met. She wanted to say something, but she was afraid. She didn't tell me anything but handed me this slip. So, what is written in it?'

'Don't you wind around like Chacha Chowdhury's nephew. Come to the point, what's written here?' Jaivardhan told Dada.

'This says, "*Bhool hoye geche, Baba. Aamake khoma kore dao aar aama ke ekhan theke niye cholo*",' said Dada, folding the paper.

'You read it bang on! *Ekdum chapsand*, just like a Bengali! Absolutely brilliant. Now kindly translate it into Hindi too,' I teased Dada.

'It's some girl who's written to her father that she's made a mistake. She's asking him to forgive her and rescue her from there,' Dada said, thoughtfully.

'Rescue her! Rescue her from where?' Jaivardhan asked.

'From Manduadih.' Dada sighed deeply.

'Manduadih! That's a . . .?' Something dawned on Jaivardhan.

'Yes, it's a red-light area,' Dada said.

'*Ram Teri Ganga Maili* was shot there! I've seen it,' I said.

'Oh! You were the one sitting in Mandakini's lap all through the movie, weren't you? You're a dumbass, fucking *champak*. Can't you stay shut for a while?' Dada was serious.

'What else did she say?' Dada asked the man.

'Nothing, Bhaiya. She was just crying. When I said something, she didn't understand. When she said something, I couldn't understand. I'm not upset about my money, but her tears really saddened me.'

'Can you recognize her?' Dada asked.

'Yes, Bhaiya. They all stand in line, I'll recognize her.'

'Come,' Dada said.

'Where?' I asked.

'Manduadih.'

'Have you gone mad? Do you even know what you're saying?'

'If you don't want to go, don't go. I'm definitely going.'

'I won't go anyway, and you two can't either. We have Abhay Kumar and Varma Sir's classes, and our attendance is low in both. You have to attend them,' I said with a smile.

'That's why you won't go. You'll attend these classes and give attendance for both of us as well,' Jaivardhan, who had been silent till now, said.

'How will I give attendance for both of you?' I asked, despite knowing the answer.

'Just like you have been doing for one and a half years:

Roll number 27: Yes, Sir.
29: Present, Sir.
44: Yes, Sir,' Dada mimicked.

'Listen guys, please don't go. This doesn't seem right to me,' I tried one last time.

'You get going. You're going to be late for class. See you in the evening,' Dada said and the two of them left with the man.

* * *

'How do we go?' Jaivardhan asked.

'Let's take a train from Cantt,' Dada said.

'No, Bhaiya, you get an auto to Manduadih near BHU Hospital. It'll take you straight to Shivdaspur,' the man said, who by now had told them that his name was Narhari. The three took an auto from Sir Sundarlal Hospital, which was also called BHU Hospital, and got off there directly.

The market was at some distance from the stand. It looked like an ordinary market, but the place they were headed to was a lane, a very narrow lane. Rain had made the muddy roads slippery. At the foot of the lane, on one side, there was a shop selling audio cassettes and playing loud music, while on the other was a utensil store. The environment changed completely from here on. Every house in the lane ahead looked like a dark storeroom. Four to five girls were standing in a line in front of every house, talking among themselves.

After crossing three to four storeroom-like structures, the three reached the last building. Narhari stopped at a distance and gestured towards a girl. She was wearing a red salwar-kurta. There was a wound on her head around which flies were buzzing. She was clearly upset. Narhari stopped Dada when he took a step forward.

'Not like this, Bhaiya. You see the baldish man, standing there at the paan shop? We'll have to talk to him first. Just show him the "goat" you want. He'll say 200 rupees at first but will settle for 50.'

'Goat!' Jaivardhan was stunned.

'Yes, that's what they are called here,' Narhari said.

Dada was just about to move forward when Jaivardhan stopped him.

'I'm not feeling well, let's go back to the hostel.'

'But . . . ' Dada wanted to go where the man was.

'Bhai, no. I feel really unwell.' Jaivardhan was getting nauseous.

'Yes, Bhaiya. Let's go back if he isn't feeling well. My job is done, Bhaiya. You please see if you can help in any way,' Narhari said.

* * *

After sitting in class for full five hours, one's body and mind both stop working. This becomes even more difficult when you have to attend class alone, without your friends, and mark their attendance as well. My mind was more in Manduadih than in the class anyway, so I was feeling even more bored than usual. Thinking I would talk to Shikha, I came quickly to the hostel after class was over. When I entered the room, what I saw was very unusual. Jaivardhan was asleep on my bed, covered with my blanket. Two tablets of Avomine were kept next to him. On the other bed, Dada was sitting with his head in his hands.

'How did the investigation go?' I asked.

'Are you making fun of us?' Dada asked without lifting his head.

'I'm not laughing at you, I'm proxying attendance for you. Anyway, forget this argument and tell me, what happened today?' I said, pulling at the blanket.

'Haven't been feeling well since I saw the condition there,' Dada said.

'And did you see the girl?'

'Yes. She was standing in the line like an animal, and do you know what they're called? Goats.'

'Do you know, Bengali women are often called Ma. Durga Ma, Kali Ma, Maashi Ma, Didi Ma. And here, what is that same person called? Goat! Chhi! How can a human sink so low?' Dada said softly.

'Listen, that paper had a phone number, right? Call her home. Her family will come and take her,' I remembered suddenly.

'I did. They replied saying they didn't have a daughter and hung up.'

'Looks like her family has severed relations, then.'

'Hmm, looks like it.'

'Man, when the family also doesn't care, then why should we poke our nose in their affair? We've come here to study and even that isn't working out,' I said.

'If studying isn't working out, then at least this can,' Jaivardhan said, getting up.

'Look man, why should we get into this unnecessarily?' I said.

'If this is unnecessary, then unnecessary it is. Yaar, she's someone's daughter and if we hadn't seen her, maybe we could have left her there. But we've seen her and now we can't . . .we can't leave her there,' Jaivardhan said.

'So, you went, right? I refused, but . . . ' I said.

'Man, I had lost my mind! I went off my rocker! Anything else you want to hear?' Jaivardhan shouted.

Jaivardhan's voice had become so loud that the people outside thought that a fight was underway. Navenduji and Roshan both came rushing.

'What happened? We could hear your voice outside,' Navenduji said, entering the room.

'Look at them, Navenduji. There's some girl stuck in Manduadih, and these two are insisting on rescuing her. Now, is this our job?' I told Navenduji.

'Wow! This is just what I had come to say. This topic was hot in Roshan Bhai's room as well. Some boy from Birla Hostel went there; he's Roshan Bhai's friend. He met the girl; her name is Rimpa. Her condition isn't good, she will have to be rescued from there soon. Dada and I have just spoken to an NGO about this.'

'NGO? What did you tell them?' Roshan said, wincing, as if this had displeased him.

'Look, it is impossible to rescue that girl alone from the . . . ' Navenduji had not even finished his sentence when I interrupted.

'That's what I am saying! This is something that's been going on for years. This isn't a movie where one girl can just be rescued from there!' I pointed out.

'No, no, that place is impossible to escape from even in movies. In *Mahanadhi*, Kamal Haasan's daughter . . . '

Navenduji was just about to deviate from the topic when Jaivardhan reminded him, 'Navenduji, the train is going from the tracks to the field.'

'Huh? Oh, yes, yes.' Navenduji collected himself and said, 'I mean, it's not possible to rescue just one girl from there. There's an NGO called Bitiya which works to educate children of sex workers there. That area can be raided with help from the police and that NGO. The people there will think it's a police raid. As many girls as possible will have to be saved and seated in the NGO buses. The NGO members will arrange two buses with a Bum Bole banner. The girls will have to be taken to the vehicles without losing time, and we'll have to leave before anyone understands anything. That's how that girl can be released too,' Navenduji said.

'So, why with the NGO's help? There are so many of you, you can do it alone too,' Roshan said, a bit annoyed.

'Roshan Bhai, the people from the NGO visit that area a lot. They teach their children, so entering will be easier for them,' Navenduji explained.

'No, I don't like this idea. Other people do all the work and an NGO gets all the credit!' Roshan was vexed.

'Bro, we don't need any credit-*shredit*. That's good for the NGO. Our job is to save the girl, that's it,' Dada said determinedly.

'Man, this is their area! Why do we have to get into this?' I asked.

'Their area meaning, whose area?' Roshan asked awkwardly.

'Meaning the criminals,' Dada said, handling the situation. 'It's a criminal area, that's why we're involving the police. This whole matter will be from the NGO, and we will just be volunteers. This way, we can save that girl as well.'

'Look, I'm saying this again. You people should do this yourself. Why would you let an NGO reap the benefits of your efforts?' Roshan said, looking at Navenduji.

'You people! What do you mean by you people? Are you not with us?' Jaivardhan asked.

'No. I have to leave for Kanpur today,' Roshan said.

'Oh! If you're not with us then why are you sharing your pearls of wisdom? Let us do what we're doing. We need your support now, not your counselling,' Jaivardhan said.

Roshan had already been sceptical, and Jaivardhan's taunts had given him more reason. He stood up in a huff and left the room. Navenduji got up to stop him, but Dada pulled at his hand and sat him down. After some moments of silence, Navenduji said, 'What's happened to this guy? He was all right a while ago, was saying Dada and his friends are doing good work. Suddenly heard about the NGO and got put off.'

'Someone from an NGO must have screwed him over.' Jaivardhan made a sly innuendo, as he was wont to do. Everyone had just started to laugh when I expressed my doubts.

'Why get involved with the police, bhai? Even without the police, can't we . . . ' Dada interrupted me before I could complete my sentence: 'Man, you've reached your second year of law, and you still can't understand the fact that we may have to force these girls into the bus, which would be illegal and we could be charged with trafficking in the future. That's why we need to have the police with us. And the police will do nothing but help when the people from the NGO accompany us.'

'But . . . ' I hawed.

'Three words that need to go—and, but, so. You don't even have to explain it to him, Dada. I've understood that a group of boys from the hostel will go there and carry out the raid. The police and the NGO will be there. We will raid and they'll think it was the police, so there'll be fewer chances of retaliation. It's a good plan,' Jaivardhan added.

'One more thing. Only Dada, Jaivardhan and the boy from Birla recognize that girl, Rimpa. Jaivardhan has an issue with the environment there, so he can't go. The boy from Birla went and spoke to her yesterday. He asked her name as well, so he can also come under suspicion. So, when the raid's going on, everyone else will be with their groups, but Dada, you will be alone, and you will somehow bring the girl to the bus. All right?' Navenduji asked Dada.

'Yes, all right,' Dada replied.

'It's risky, yaar. Very risky,' I said.

'That's why we're not taking you. You sit here and listen to Akhtaribai Faizabadi's melodies,' Dada retorted.

'And Dada won't go alone. I will also be there,' Jaivardhan said.

'So, should I sit here in the hostel and peel jackfruit? I will also come die with you,' I said.

* * *

Shivdaspur—the largest red-light area of Banaras. Nothing was different in Shivdaspur that day, certainly not for its residents. A group of street singers passed by intermittently, calling out 'Bol-Bam!' The atmosphere of Shivdaspur got better as evening dawned.

The groups of girls outside each building were looking at every passer-by longingly. There was more chaos than usual that day. Rickshaw drivers, truck drivers and labourers often came to the market after a day's labour, but that day there was a larger crowd of young men. This could have struck the ever-alert minds of the owner of the market and the pimps, but the election rally happening alongside kept them distracted. Someone even asked, 'Arre, guru! Why are you here?'

'Oh, I came here for the minister's rally, so from there . . . ' Jaivardhan's answer cleared their doubts.

Alankar, Navendu, Nepali, Vineet, seniors and juniors were all roaming around with their groups, but the three of us were facing the biggest problems.

'That's her! Right in the middle, wearing the green salwar-kurta,' Dada said.

'Yes, but the problem is that this is the last building on the lane. The road in front is a dead end. There's only one way we can run—the way we came from. And the bus is at least 150 metres from here,' Jaivardhan said.

'Which means, if we get stuck, they won't even find our bodies,' Dada whispered.

'Look, we can't take her until she comes with us herself. She's not a child whom we can just carry,' Jaivardhan whispered back.

'Okay, listen, do you see the bald guy there? Go and talk to him about money. Till then, we'll talk to the girl, and if something works out, we'll walk slowly towards the bus. If the raid signal comes amid all this, then don't run, just leave calmly or the bald fucker will suspect something. Somehow, by talking or by force, I'll get her to the bus,' Dada said.

Dada and I then started walking towards the girl. By then, Jaivardhan had reached the pimp.

He immediately said brashly, 'That one in the green suit.'

'It'll be Rs 600 for a cottage and Rs 1000 for a hotel,' the bald guy replied.

'It's not that much. It's 400. I won't take much time.' Jaivardhan was getting him tied up in conversation.

'No, 400 won't be enough. Won't be possible below 600.' The bald pimp was adamant.

Meanwhile, Dada and I had reached the girl, who was behaving just like the others. Even as we were walking towards her, Dada asked, '*Tomar naam ki?*' She stayed silent and did not give us her name. Suddenly a girl pretended to fall over me. I jumped, scared. The girls started to laugh. Everything we knew about such places came from movies. It was also awkward to bump into friends of ours who had been assigned the task of taking other girls to the bus. I was really getting uneasy, but Dada wasn't uncomfortable in the least. We reached the girl. '*Aapni Bangali?*' Dada asked her softly. Who knows what she made of it, but the girl just lifted five fingers on her right hand and one on her left. Dada realized that she was talking about money. He gestured towards Jaivardhan.

'Abey, what is she trying to say?' I asked Dada.

'She's scared. She's talking about paying the pimp. I told her that Jaivardhan is talking about the money,' Dada whispered.

'Oh,' I said.

Dada gestured to her to accompany him, and she started following him slowly.

Jaivardhan, on the other hand, had engrossed the pimp in conversation, but as soon as he saw that the girl was going somewhere, he asked Jaivardhan, 'Are those two people with you?'

'No, do you think I've brought my entire family here with me?' Jaivardhan shot back.

'Stay here for a minute!' The pimp had become suspicious. He ran behind Dada and me.

Right before the bald guy could reach us, the NGO volunteer gave the signal for the raid. The groups of boys from the hostel got busy trying to save the girls. Dada pulled the girl into the bus. She got scared and started to cry. The other girls were also unprepared for this situation. Some even struggled, broke free and rushed back into their dark cottages, locking the doors behind them. The volunteers succeeded in forcefully pushing some into the bus. If a third person were to look at it, this appeared more like an attack than a rescue. This attack was, however, to rescue the girls from a trap. There was chaos all around; it did not feel any different from a riot. Everyone in the market was trying to stay alive and run. The moment I sat in the bus, I remembered Jaivardhan.

I saw him, trapped in the tumult, trying to run towards the bus.

'Jaivardhan, run!' I screamed as I saw him approach, but by then the bus had taken off and everything soon disappeared in a cloud of dust. Jaivardhan vanished from my view. For a moment, the world came to a pause. The girls were scared. They were shouting. They were abusing us. Everyone was brought to the police station, where our statements were taken as well. After the investigation was over, we thanked the people from the NGO and returned to the hostel.

* * *

We were so exhausted by the time we reached the hostel that our bodies were wracked with pain. Everyone went to their rooms and immediately fell asleep. Sleep evaded only one room—ours.

'Where's Jaivardhan, man?' I asked.

'He'll come. He couldn't get on to the bus, right . . . must be coming in an auto.' There was more reassurance in Dada's words than there was conviction.

'I saw him for a moment, then the bus took off and he vanished.'

'He'll arrive. He's a boss. Must have started explaining one of his idioms to someone. Even the seniors put in a lot of effort, or we wouldn't have been able to save so many girls,' Dada, changing the topic.

'Man! If you think of it, it's so funny . . . the whole hostel in a red-light area!' I laughed.

'Except Roshan. Anyway, why complain about him, even you weren't going at first.'

I was just about to reply when a familiar voice called out, 'Open the door, motherfuckers!' It was Jaivardhan.

'Look! Jaivardhan is here,' I brightened up as I opened the door.

'If you had to kill in my fields, you could have let me to grow some crops first, you assholes! You left me alone and ran, didn't you?' Jaivardhan laughed.

'We messed up, man. Your task was difficult. But you could have reached the bus, right?'

'Ghanta I could have reached the bus. If only Uncle would let me.' Jaivardhan was laughing and talking at once.

'What do you mean?' I asked.

'I mean that these idiots mistook me for a pimp and caught me as well,' Jaivardhan said, coughing from the exertion of laughing too much.

'What?' I asked, open-mouthed.

'Yes man, I tried to tell them that I was a student, not a pimp. But he didn't listen. Do you know what he said?' Jaivardhan asked, trying not to laugh.

'What?' Even Dada was having a fit of laughter.

'He said, if you are a student, then I'm the president.' Jaivardhan spurted with laughter, leading to another bout of coughing.

'Careful, man. How were you released, then?' I asked, handing Jaivardhan some water.

'Oh, so when they brought me to the police station, Chaubey from the NGO was sitting there. He also started laughing, but got me released,' Jaivardhan said, taking a sip.

'Chalo, thankfully you came back safe. There's one thing to be glad of: We saved someone's life,' I said.

'Ghanta you saved a life!' Jaivardhan said, waving his thumb at me.

'What?' I asked.

'You did save her, but when the police asked her name, do you know what she said?' Jaivardhan said.

'Rimpa,' I said.

'No. Jebunnisa.'

'What! What are you saying? Her name was Rimpa, right?' I asked Dada.

'Yes, man. That's what Navenduji had told me.'

'Bro, she must have given a wrong name for fear of the police,' I said.

'Yes, possibly. Anyway, at least she got out of that hell. Now if the NGO does something good then the girl's life will be saved,' Dada said.

'Who knows? I don't trust the NGO, but what can we even do?' Jaivardhan said.

'Man, we had gone with good intentions, to save someone's life. That did happen, right? Now it all depends on what fate has in store,' I said.

'Yes, now I'm also going to sleep. Either way, we have Murali Sir's extra class from 7 a.m. tomorrow,' Jaivardhan said as he left the room.

Oye Lucky, Lucky Oye

Laptop—the most important and the most harmful object of the first decade of the twenty-first century. Important, because the kind fathers of changing times viewed it as a substitute for a typewriter. They believed it was necessary to have computer skills to get a job. Just like an MBA is what a BA used to be, a computer is what a typewriter used to be. As a result, fathers fulfilled even this expensive demand their sons made. It is also a harmful object, because the first thing the son learns to use is invariably Windows Media Player. Word, Excel and PowerPoint come later, in their own time.

This wasn't entirely true for me. When there were talks of IT, I wasn't entirely unaware of it and wanted to do a master's in computer application. But this wasn't possible, and I ended up studying law. It was, however, true that I knew a little more about computers than my friends did.

I had to go home right before the second semester ended because I got sick with jaundice and could only appear for five exams, but the good part was that I got a laptop. Papa gave me a lot of instructions and also told me to keep practising typing on it. But I had been given wings and spent almost all of the next semester watching movies. And now, the third-semester exams were knocking on the door.

'Fucker, your studies have gone to the dogs! Ever since you got the laptop, all you do is watch movies. The exams are almost here, you'll pass everything else, but CrPC will trip you up,' Jaivardhan fumed.

'And this guy has fucked me over as well. Just watches movies himself and makes us watch them too!' Dada agreed.

'Since you're so busy watching movies, raja, go write about movies in your CrPC exam! You've passed only five exams in your second-semester exams anyway!' Jaivardhan told me.

'I didn't pass only five exams, I took only five exams because of jaundice.'

'Oh, look! This man talks as well! Don't you talk, Raja Banaras, focus on watching movies! You'll miss a scene. Look! Dalip Tahil is getting beaten up! Got a bioscope and now he's got his ass stuck to it all day. And what about everything your father did for you? Goodbye, huh?' Jaivardhan bristled.

'You're not getting it, Baba. It's not substantive law where you can write anything and pass. We haven't attended classes anyway, and it's really tough too,' Dada tried to explain.

'Now let him be. Dalip Tahil will write his paper for him and Bruce Lee will check it. Our papers have to checked by Moor-li, not Bruce Lee. Come, let's get some revision done, otherwise we're both going to fail with him,' Jaivardhan told Dada.

'Nobody is going to fail.'

'Why, huh? Is Bruce Lee Sir setting the paper?' Jaivardhan taunted.

'No, Murali Sir,' I answered quickly.

'Now look at that! This is absolutely breaking news! Did you receive this news from your black buffalo as well?' Jaivardhan called the laptop a buffalo.

'That's the problem. Murali Sir is setting the paper. He's going to ask exactly what he has taught and we have no idea what he's taught! How many classes have we even gone for? Damn it, there's an attendance issue as well. I have no idea if it'll reach 75 per cent or not!' Dada started panting as he spoke.

'The papers will be with us before the exam,' I said confidently.

'Bhai, Babva has lost it! He's watched too many detective films, don't waste your time on him. I'm telling you, let's go do some revision.' Jaivardhan was losing patience now.

'Let's hear him out. And you're talking about revision as if we've studied anything in the first place. Have you studied anything? What are you going to revise? Haan bey, you go on. So, Baba, how will we get the papers?' Dada asked me.

'Have you ever looked at Murali Sir's assignments?' I asked them.

'Yes, what's so special about them?' Dada asked.

'All the assignments are typed in a particular font: Tahoma,' I said.

'So?' Dada was eager for me to get to the point.

'What is typed in four pages in Tahoma, fits in fewer pages in Times New Roman. Tahoma is often used by those people who don't know how to change the font, meaning novices who have just bought computers or laptops, people over forty years of age or people who know just enough about computers and typing to get by,' I finished.

'Oh! So that means Murali Sir is new to typing.' Dada lit a cigarette.

'But what's the connection with our question paper?' Jaivardhan, who had been listening quietly so far, asked.

'There is a connection, a deep connection. Murali Sir has to give the 15 August speech in Hindi, and he's obviously going to get someone else to write it for him. All you have to do is somehow let Murali Sir know that my Hindi skills are good. And you know that Telugu boy? Our junior, Ravishankar! Send him to me.'

'Baba is talking nonsense,' Jaivardhan muttered as he left. He knew that Murali Sir had to give the 15 August speech in Hindi. If Murali Sir would speak to anyone about this, it would be Kamlesh, who had topped both semesters. So, he went straight to the library and sat down at the table right behind Kamlesh. He started talking to the boy next to him. 'All kinds of talented people come to BHU, each *dhurandhar* better than the other.'

The other boy was not at all interested in this, but Jaivardhan had already ragged him so he had no option but to listen. Jaivardhan kept talking: 'Just last year, Suraj got an award from the governor. He doesn't talk about it but turned out he was the one who wrote the Jharkhand governor's first speech. And he's translated Dostoevsky's *White Nights* into Hindi, I've read it myself.' Jaivardhan continued to talk without realizing that this boy knew neither Dostoevsky nor the governor.

What Jaivardhan did realize, however, was that Kamlesh knew them well. After listening for a while, Kamlesh got up and left the library. Jaivardhan could not figure out whether or not Kamlesh had heard what him. At that moment, the boy asked, 'Bhaiya, who is this Suraj?'

'Shut up! Have you come here to the library to listen to stories? Where do you live, Sir? No context nor question, but hey, the groom is my son! Study, my friend, study. This is what will help you later! You have your whole life ahead of you to listen to stories!' Jaivardhan left the boy grappling with the meaning of the proverb and walked out of the library.

Ravishankar was also on his way to my room. It wasn't hard for Dada to get favours from the juniors—after all, he was the only senior who shared his cigarettes. The others just smoked theirs themselves.

'Sir, did you need anything?' Ravishankar asked as soon as he entered the room.

'No, nothing much, Ravi. Come, sit,' I said.

'And, how's work going, man?' I started a conversation.

'It's all right, Sir. I only have trouble with Family Law.'

'Yes, a lot of Farsi has been used in Family Law, that's why. It tends to be tough for non-Hindi speakers. You take Navenduji's notes,' I said.

'Yes, Sir, Telugu-speaking people do have some difficulty with Hindi.'

'Oh, yes! Telugu reminds me. I have a Telugu friend. She wants to message to someone saying, "Please don't ask for secret, official, personal question and document." How do you write this in Telugu, man?'

'*Dayachosi swantvaina, rahasyamaina, prashnalukayatalu adgaavaddu,*' Ravi spit it out in a single breath.

'*Baap re*! Anyway, you write it down. I'll type it and send the message.'

'Now do you see how hard it is for us to understand Hindi?' Ravishankar laughed as he wrote it on a piece of paper and left the room.

As soon as he left, Jaivardhan entered and said, 'I've done your job, Baba. Haven't worked as much on writing an exam as I have on cooking up this storm! Kamlesh must have been heard me, he was sitting right in front. Now let's see, if only something happens! Come, let's go get some Maggi or something. My uncle from Hyderabad Gate, he cooks such A-class Maggi!' Jaivardhan said as he took the key to Dada's bike.

'You go. I've just got a CD today, I have to return it by evening,' I said.

'Just go die, man! Why weren't you just born in China, huh? You'd find Bruce Lee, Chuce Lee, all the Lees there. It's the bioscope that's tripped you up, right? You'll be left with no scope in life, I tell you. Baba gets a buffalo, now it'll trot where he goes!' Jaivardhan started the bike and rode off, still shouting at me.

Dada was sleeping. He woke up when he heard the sound of the bike. He threw off his blanket, quickly ran outside, then came in again.

'Where did my bike go?'

'Huh?' I could not hear anything because of my earphones.

'Who took my bike?' Dada asked loudly.

'I can't hear anything, speak louder!'

'You motherfucker, you have an effing wire in your ears! You'll be able to hear when you take it out!' Dada said as he yanked out my earphone. 'Who took my bike?'

'Jaivardhan,' I said, pausing the film.

'Oh! Then it's all right. I dreamt that someone was stealing my bike and I was eating Maggi,' Dada said, rubbing his eyes.

'Even when you dream you're thinking about the bike! *Saala*, dream of Demi Moore, of Kate Winslet, of Meg Ryan! Don't worry so much about the bike. And do you think I'll let your bike get stolen from the hostel?' I said, playing the film again.

'That's the problem, Baba! Even if your wife runs away, you'll wait for the movie to end first,' Dada said as he gargled, and then shouted loudly, 'Bho . . . le . . . na . . . th!'

This was the evening call to play cricket. With this one alarm, the entire cricket team of juniors would collect and the field would be set.

My movie had ended by the time Dada came in after the game.

'Wanna go have tea?' Dada asked, yawning.

'Come,' I said, putting on a T-shirt.

'The juniors are all crazy. The exams are approaching and all of them showed up to play cricket. Can't even refuse when someone comes to your door,' Dada explained himself.

'Yes, totally! And it was Ganesha looking for his father with all those calls of Bholenath, wasn't it?' I retaliated.

'What's wrong with that? Now is it wrong to take God's name?' Dada picked up a samosa as soon as we reached the store.

'No, my man. Take it, take the name as much as you can. That's when Bholenath will read your application, isn't it?' I said as I sipped my tea.

'Oh, application reminds me! There was a registered post in your name.' Dada picked up another samosa.

'Must be a rakhi.' I finished my tea.

'Haan, *sasur*! You have a sister in the Staff Selection Commission office sending you rakhis, huh? It's an interview letter,' Dada said, taking it out of his pocket.

'Are you kidding me?' I said, pouncing on the letter.

'Do I look like a court jester to you? It's an interview letter for section officer.' Dada took out some money.

'Let it go, man, I'll pay today. I'm in a good mood.' I held his hand back.

'Baba, the day you become an officer, we'll eat biryani and drink vodka. Don't you settle it with a cup of tea,' Dada said as he paid.

'Arey yaar! The interview is on the 14th!' I said surprised. 'And today is the 10th already!'

'What a great postal department we have! Gave us the letter ten days late!' Dada said. I was just looking at the envelope after taking it from Dada, when someone called out to me.

'Suraj! Suraj!'

I looked back; it was Murali Sir. Both of us approached him, bowed slightly in greeting and then stood with our hands behind our backs.

'And, how studies be going?' Murali Sir asked in his unique way.

'Yes, good Sir,' we chorused.

'Anurag, you be having to play less cricket. Exams be coming. Go, go study.' Murali Sir sent Dada off.

'Yes, Sir,' Dada said and proceeded to the hostel.

Now Murali Sir addressed me.

'Suraj, why don't you be sitting in the front row in class?'

'The front bench gets full early, Sir.' I gave an excuse.

'Which means you be coming late to class?' Murali Sir retorted.

It was better to stand quietly than say anything more.

'Look Suraj, this year be very important for you. Study with all your heart. This is your last bus, if it be going by, it be getting hard.' Murali Sir lectured. 'Give some time to your work. I have read your project, you are being a good student.'

Murali Sir was going on and on, and I wondered if this was how he spoke to all his students. I woke up with a start when he changed the topic: 'Roshan was telling me that your Hindi is good.'

'Sir, it's all right,' I said.

'No, no. You are be acting modest. You've even got an award for Hindi from Rajyapal.'

'Yes, Sir.' I had nothing else to say. Now I realized what storm Jaivardhan had been talking about.

'Listen, 15 August is about to arrive and I have no time at all. Could you please write something about 15 August in Hindi for me?'

'With pleasure, Sir.' I couldn't say anything beyond this. Not even that I had an interview in Delhi on the 14.

'Here's a pen drive. Please save it in this and be giving to me by the 14th so I can look through it.'

I was shocked to see the pen drive in Murali Sir's hand. I think Murali Sir saw my confusion and said, 'I don't be understanding this pen drive-pencil drive business. Roshan gave it to me and said I can use it to transfer data. Please be making sure it doesn't get lost.'

'Don't worry, Sir. I'll keep it carefully,' I said, dispelling Murali Sir's fears.

'Thank you, Suraj! Go, study, the exams are approaching, and please don't make the garden into a cricket ground,' Murali Sir laughed.

I came straight back to the hostel after meeting Murali Sir. Dada and Jaivardhan were already there in the room, playing chess.

'Dude, what did Murali Sir say?' Jaivardhan asked.

'He was asking me to study,' I replied, taking off my T-shirt.

'Wow, what's new in that? He even tells Tommy the same thing.' Jaivardhan was referring to the hostel dog.

'And he asked me to write a speech in Hindi for him,' I said, gathering the certificates I needed for my interview.

'Very good, my son! The job is done. You're about to checkmate, Baba!' Jaivardhan practically lifted me up.

'What job? Baba's going to Delhi to give an interview,' Dada said, clearing up the board.

'What?' Jaivardhan said, throwing me down.

'Meaning, someone brought a cup but the coffee machine doesn't have a plug. Listen, Baba. You aren't going for any interview or any nonsense. It's the effing first time everything is going right here, and you're going off to Delhi! What will you get by giving an interview, huh? You've given so many interviews before, and what happened? You return with your mouth to the south. Listen, Dada, this guy isn't going for any interviews. He has something going on with someone in Delhi. Otherwise, you tell me, otherwise why would he take a pillow with him every time? He might forget his clothes, he might forget his food, but he'll never ever forget his pillow! Why do you carry that pillow, huh?' Jaivardhan said, frowning.

'I can't sleep without a pillow, so I take it with me. I have to take the interview because the exam went well. Just because I didn't get selected in interviews earlier doesn't mean I won't get selected in this one either,' I said, zipping my bag.

'So, they boasted an elephant had come, but when I went to see it was only a pup! Nothing can be done now. Baba has become an officer, so Dada, let's go get some revision done.' Jaivardhan was disappointed.

'Who said nothing can be done now? Everything will get done and it'll be done just fine. You two just keep revising,' I said, putting my hand on Jaivardhan's shoulder.

'Yes, Baba! You're Lord Brahma!' Jaivardhan smiled weakly and left the room.

'Which train are you taking?' Dada asked dully.

'Shiv Ganga.'

'Ticket?'

'I haven't bought one, but you usually get a seat.'

'When's your train?' Dada asked again.

'Tomorrow evening.'

'All right, let's go to sleep now. We'll talk tomorrow morning,' Dada said, covering his face with his blanket.

'You sleep, I have some work.'

'Damn you, you idiot! You and your movies!' Dada said as he pulled the blanket on to himself. I had to stay awake not to watch a movie but to write the Hindi speech. I had to arrange my clothes and pack my important documents. I didn't even realize when I fell asleep while writing the speech. I woke up only to Dada's thundering call of 'Bholenath'.

'Abey, what's the time?' I asked.

'It's already 11,' Dada replied.

'Arey, yaar!' I said waking up with a start. 'I haven't even arranged my certificates yet.'

'So what were you doing at night, drawing pictures? I'm going to the mess to eat.'

'Ask them to send the food to the room,' I said, arranging my bag.

By the time I ate and packed my bag, it was time to leave. That's when I called Shikha. Like always, she asked me to be alert during the journey, to keep my certificates carefully and wished me luck. She said everything but the words I wanted to hear: I love you. Anyway, I was just about to get ready and leave when Dada entered the room after playing cricket.

'What time is the train?' Dada asked.

'7 p.m.,' I said, lifting the bag on to my shoulder.

'Come, I'll drop you,' Dada said as he picked up his keys.

Dada parked the bike after reaching Cantt. He took a platform ticket and accompanied me inside. The train was on time. I was just about to get on it when Dada said, 'Don't take what Jaivardhan said to heart. *Parphandi hai saala*; he's got too much of an attitude. And do well in the interview. Make eye contact with the interviewer, you look down a lot. Don't worry about CrPC. Come after the interview, we'll prepare for that shit in two days.'

'Keep your phone switched on.' I hugged Dada and boarded the train.

* * *

I reached the SSC office at 8 a.m. on 14 August. I checked my name on the notice board, then stepped away from the other boys and called up Dada.

'Yes, what's up?' Dada asked as he picked up the phone.

'Where are you?'

'In the room, bhai. Jaivardhan's doing his revision. Where are you?'

'In the SSC office. Forget about me, you do as I say. There must be a pen drive underneath my pillow, take it out.'

'Yes, there is. Taken it out. What happened, Baba? Is everything all right?' Dada got worried.

'Everything is all right. Now you go quickly to Murali Sir.'

'What?' Dada was dumbfounded 'What will I get by going to Murali Sir?'

'Don't ask questions. There is no time. I've spoken to Murali Sir. He knows that the speech I have written is in the pen drive. You go alone, leave Jaivardhan in the hostel. And listen, don't disconnect the call, I'll disconnect it when I have to.'

Dada left Jaivardhan in the room and reached Murali Sir's house, which was adjacent to the hostel.

'Come, Anurag, Suraj was just telling me that he had to go to Delhi for an interview but he was be leaving the speech with you,' Murali Sir said.

'Yes, Sir, it is on the pen drive. Suraj is also on call.'

'Ask Sir where his computer is,' I told Dada.

'Sir, where is your computer?' Dada asked.

'Come, it is be here. I am not understanding this pen drive, pencil drive. You please transfer,' Murali Sir said.

'I've put in the pen drive, which file is it?' Dada asked me.

'It's a file called "15 August". Place your cursor over each file one by one. Open the one at the very end. Keep rotating the cursor. Now I'm disconnecting the call and calling Jaivardhan. I'll speak to you in a couple of minutes,' I told Dada.

'Hello, Jaivardhan.'

'Yes Baba, what are you trying to do?'

'Listen, Jaivardhan, where are you standing?'

'Outside your room. That's where Dada left me.'

'Who's passing by in front of you?'

'Vijay Brother,' he said again, looking at Vijay.

'Punch him.'

'What? Have you lost it? Why should I punch Vijay Brother?'

'Just punch him,' I said hurriedly.

'But . . . ' Jaivardhan was contemplating.

'Just do what I'm telling you to, and do it fast,' I scolded.

'All right, I punched him. Go on,' was Jaivardhan's next reply. From what I heard on the phone, it seemed like Jaivardhan had punched him hard.

'Now abuse him and punch him again. I'm disconnecting the call,' I said and cut the phone. I walked around for a while and then called Dada.

'Dada, what's up?'

'Abey, something crazy is up! Someone has punched someone in the hostel, that's where Murali Sir has gone.'

'Great! Now listen. First, open C drive and type the words "*swant, swantvaina, rahasya, rahasyamaina, prashn, question, prashnaalu, kayatalu*" into the search box one by one.

'Why? Dude, what the fuck are you making me do?'

'Swantvaina, rahasyamaina, prashnaalu, kayatalu,' I said again.

'Say it again, slowly.' Dada was not able to understand anything.

'Swantvaina, rahasyamaina, prashnaalu, kayatalu, look quickly.'

'I'm looking, man! Just let me breathe a little. Yes . . . yes! Yes, there is something!' Dada said happily.

'Great! Now, copy all the files that are upto 400 KB.'

'It's taking time, dude! This damn computer is so slow. Even the fight seems to have ended,' Dada was getting worried.

'It'll get done, don't worry,' I assured him.

'It's done!' Dada said.

'All right, I'm hanging up now. It's time for certificate verification,' I said and cut the call.

'This Jaivardhan boy is always getting into fights,' Murali Sir said as he entered the room.

'What happened, Sir?' Dada asked.

'Nothing. Has he written that speech?'

'Yes, Sir, I've put that into your computer. Come, I'll show you,' Dada said as he took the pen drive out.

'It's all right, it's in the computer, I'll be seeing it in a while. Thank you. The pen drive is Roshan's, give it to him,' Murali Sir told Dada.

'Yes, Sir,' Dada said and left with the pen drive.

* * *

'What happened, dude? What's the chaos about?' Dada asked Jaivardhan after reaching the hostel.

'Oh, man. Baba called and told me to punch Vijay Brother. So I punched him. Then he asked me to abuse him and then punch him. When I started kicking him, everyone called Murali Sir. Now Murali Sir asked, why be you punching him? What could I say to that? I thought I will call and ask why "I be punching", but Baba's phone was busy. What could I even tell Murali Sir?' Jaivardhan said in one breath.

'Baba's made some big plans. Come, let's go to the room,' Dada laughed.

'Ghanta he's made big plans. Suddenly asks me to punch Vijay Brother. Poor thing was swinging his arms, full Dev Anand style. Then he asks me to punch him more! How can I punch someone who's already down? But I hit him anyway. Just when I was about to ask him what to do, he hung up!' Jaivardhan said, feeling bad for Vijay Brother.

'So Baba made you do this to call Murali Sir here so I could copy the file,' Dada said, using his brains.

'Oh! Did you find anything?' Jaivardhan had now forgotten his woe for Vijay Brother.

'Well, I have copied it. Now let's wait for his call,' Dada said.

'Let's go eat. There's chhole bhature in the mess today,' Jaivardhan said as he got up.

'They're training us to be horses here, not lawyers. Only horses eat so much chana,' Dada said, and both got ready to go to the mess.

'And what will you do if we find Vijay Brother in the mess?' Dada joked.

'I'll apologize, what else?' Jaivardhan rested his head on Dada's shoulder.

I, on the other hand, had returned to my hotel after giving the interview. I was so exhausted I fell asleep in the evening. When I woke up at night, I saw that it was 10 p.m. Shikha had told me to call her immediately after the interview, but I had forgotten because of all the stress. I quickly started dialling her number, but before I could call Shikha, Dada called me.

'Bhai, how was the interview?' Dada asked despite knowing the answer.

'It was all right. There was a board of men, wasn't too effective,' I joked.

'Never mind, it'll work out. When are you coming?'

'I'll be there tomorrow,' I replied, arranging my bag.

'What do I do about the pen drive?' Dada was getting eager.

'Let me come tomorrow, we'll open it then.'

'Who's going to wait till tomorrow? I'm already swelling up from the waiting I've done all morning. And Murali Sir

has said we need to return the pen drive to Roshan as well,'
Jaivardhan said.

'You asses, you've put the phone on speaker? Turn off
the speaker, quick! Our room is a community space anyway,
people keep walking in all the time.'

'Here! I've turned off the speaker. Now tell me,'
Jaivardhan said impatiently.

'Put the pen drive into the laptop port,' I said.

'Eh? Put what . . . where?' Jaivardhan fumbled.

'You idiot, pass the phone to Dada!' I said, annoyed.

'Yes, yes, take it, Dada! You figure out this rocket
science. Only a bird understands the call of a bird!'
Jaivardhan passed the phone to Dada.

'Put the pen drive in the port and open it,' I repeated.

'Opened. Now?'

'First, double click on the question file.'

'Done.'

'What happened?' It was my turn to get impatient.

'It didn't open,' Dada said slowly.

'Dude, double click it!'

'Listen, don't you teach me how to open files. I've
already understood what a genius you are,' Dada snapped.

'*Maafi, malik*! But why isn't it opening? Does it say
something when you try?'

'Yes, it says enter password to open file.'

'Fuck, dude!' I could think of nothing else to say.

'What happened, Baba? What's all this fucktalk about?
Is there a big problem?'

'Murali Sir is more computer-savvy than we thought. He's protected the file with a password.'

'What now?'

'One thing is for certain, the questions are in this file.'

'Then? We'll have to do something, we can't give up after coming so close!' Dada sounded upset.

'We'll have to spend.'

'Spend? How much?' Dada asked.

'88 dollars. We'll have to buy a password cracker.'

'88 dollars as in?' Dada asked again.

'As in 4000 rupees.'

'Jaivardhan is saying that if he had dollars, then there's no reason he would be friends with you. Give us a cheap, viable solution.'

'Then nothing can be done.'

'All right, let's keep the dollar thing as the last option, but think of something else.' Dada was not one to give up easily.

'Brute force method won't work. Dictionary method won't work . . . RTF method also won't work. Random access . . . hold on, hold on! Check, which version of MS Word it is?'

'It's MS Word 2003,' Dada told me immediately.

'*Badhiya*! God is with us. Now check, is there something called Hex Editor on the desktop?'

'Hex Editor? Hex Editor . . . yes, it's here,' Dada replied instantly.

'Open it.'

'Opened it. Now?'

'Now open that file in Hex Editor.'

'Opened. Oh, dude! It's opening in something like binary. One whole page. I can't understand anything.'

'All right, go to the very bottom of that page and see— can you see an exclamation sign?' This was my last attempt.

'In the first line at the end, yes, I can see an exclamation sign in the last binary.' There was hope in Dada's voice.

'What's written before that?'

'E9 CC B3 88. This is what's written.'

'Just make these into 00s and save the file.'

'Saved it, Sir, what next?' Dada said hopefully.

'Now take the name of Bholenath and open the file.'

'Boom!' When I heard Dada's voice, I thought my eardrums would burst.

'Abey, what happened?' I asked impatiently.

'What are you doing LAW for, my friend? You should have been in RAW. It opened, dude! It really is the paper! There are thirty-two questions in the three-hour paper! We would have been screwed in the exam. Here, Jaivardhan wants to speak to you.' Dada gave Jaivardhan the phone.

'Baba, you are great! You are great, Baba! Dude, I couldn't have thought . . . ' Jaivardhan was really happy.

'All right now, let me sleep.'

'It's not like I'm pulling your blanket away from you! I'm just saying that everything has been going well from the beginning. Now wait, you'll get selected also.'

'Let's hope for the best,' I said. 'And how is everything going well, huh? You had to tell Kamlesh, you told Roshan Chaudhuri instead? Is this what's going well?'

'Roshan Chaudhuri?' Jaivardhan asked, shocked.

'Of course! That's what Murali Sir told me.'

'Arre! I had told Kamlesh, Baba! Ghanta Murali Sir's memory, doesn't remember anything. Must be calling Kamlesh Roshan. Forget the stupid conversation, you come quick. Going to treat . . . ' The phone's battery died even as Jaivardhan was speaking.

Mera Naam Joker: My Name Is Joker

'Do all of you think your lecturers and professors don't read your papers?' Pande Sir said, entering the class and putting a bundle of answer sheets on the desk.

'There you go! These look like the Constitutional Law papers. Have they been checked?' Jaivardhan said to Dada, who was sitting next to him.

'Abey, will he announce the marks in class as well?' I whispered into Dada's ear.

'Sit quietly, guys. Sir is looking at us. Anyway, we will only get marks for what we've written,' Dada said.

'If we make a compilation of all the cases you have written in your papers, it'll become an encyclopaedia of legal jokes. Why don't all of you understand that you are students of a very noble profession? If you make mistakes like these, then God only knows what will become of this country,' Pande Sir said, cleaning his glasses.

Actually, most of the people who took the exam didn't even know what the question was and what answer needed to be written. They just wrote whatever they knew. We had been attempting question papers using Dubeyji's Formula One theory anyway, which was to study only one chapter and to somehow fit it into every question. We hadn't expected the professor to conduct a post-mortem of the papers, that too in class. So, we were just hoping that these papers weren't ours. At this point, we were communicating by passing notes.

'Must be your paper?' Jaivardhan wrote to me.

'Yaar, probably isn't. I couldn't remember the name of the party, so I made something up, but all the facts were correct,' I replied in my note.

'Even I haven't written anything joke-like,' Jaivardhan wrote again.

'Then it must be Dada's paper,' I wrote. Before Dada could explain himself, Pande Sir started talking again.

'I seriously think that short notes should not be part of the question paper. First you see which four of the eight questions you can attempt, and then you definitely do one of the short notes somehow. Done and dusted, isn't it?' Pande Sir was really disappointed and angry.

'I've attempted the short notes,' I wrote.

'So have I,' Jaivardhan wrote back.

'Me too,' even Dada wrote this time.

'Almost all the papers are the same. Now, I can't read everyone's paper. Look at this one paper, though.' Pande Sir put on his glasses and said, 'So the question was: Write a short note on Amicus Curiae.

'I am reading out the answer word for word: Amicus Curiae was born in France. She was Madam Curie's cousin. When Madam Curie discovered radium, then her cousin Amicus Curie was with her. Amicus Curiae was shocked when Madam Curie did not give her name for the discovery of radium. Amicus Curiae went into shock and in this state of shock, she discovered iridium, because of which her name got permanently etched in the pages of history.' Pande Sir looked up. Laughter was already resounding through the class.

'Fifteen cases have been written in response to a different question. I wish I could read all the cases, but we don't have much time, so I am reading out two. The first case states "Bahattar Singh vs. Chihattar Singh". The facts say that Bahattar Singh had *bahattar*, seventy-two bighas of land while Chihattar Singh had seventy-six bighas. This difference of four bighas became a cause for dispute, and Bahattar Singh murdered Chihattar Singh. Bahattar Singh filed a lawsuit after being released from prison.'

'Whose paper is this?' I asked Jaivardhan, laughing.

'Whoever it is, they're full entertainment. Their marks should be full as well,' Jaivardhan said.

'Don't talk, and please pay attention,' Pande Sir said to us and continued reading. 'The second case is Tyre vs. Tube. Yes, you heard me right! The parties are B. Tyre and C. Tube. Now I'm reading the facts of this case: The plaintiff or prosecutor used to work in a tyre company. His job was to pump air into tyres. One day, suddenly, the tube of one of the tyres burst while pumping air into it, because of which the prosecutor lost his sense of hearing. He demanded compensation from the tyre company, which the company refused. This is why the lawsuit was filed.

'There are several other cases quoted. Like Handle vs. Pedal; K. Kujur vs. A. Hujur; Swagster vs. Union of India. But I don't have it in me to read out anymore.'

Pande Sir took a deep breath and continued, 'I have a request to all of you, you have nine other subjects. Constitutional Law is not the only thing you study all semester. Please distribute these cases among the other subjects too. I can't handle so much pressure alone. I earnestly request all of you to please let me remain a professor of Constitutional Law. Do not make me a psychologist. Thanks for listening.'

'Sir, whose paper is it?' a voice called from behind.

'It belongs to one of you. Thanks again.' With that Pande Sir quickly went out.

'Must be quite a man, whoever this paper belongs to!' I said, controlling my laughter.

'Come, let's go the canteen and get some tea. Damn, my body is hurting because of all the laughing.'

'Order three cups of tea,' I said.

'Just two. I'll smoke a cigarette,' Dada said. I was just getting up to order tea when someone called out, 'Suraj!'

Dubeyji was standing there, with a book in one hand and a papaya in the other.

'Arre, Dubey Baba! Come, come, want some tea?' I asked.

'No, no. I want the IPC book. Do you have it?' Dubey asked sadly.

'I do, but why are looking so down in the dumps?' I asked.

'He's given me three marks in Constitution.' Dubeyji's face fell.

'What! Three marks? Three on hundred?' Jaivardhan was even more upset than Dubeyji.

'Yes. Three on hundred. What was wrong in the Amicus Curie answer? I had studied it in class 10. Marie Curie did have a sister. This must have been her, Amicus Curie! And are village cases not considered cases? These city people think village people are fools. My father had even testified in the Bahattar Singh case. Sir just called me, said he's given me three marks, and he'll throw me out if I don't improve. Sir shouldn't have been given two subjects. I have my presentation on sedition tomorrow, that's why I need the IPC book,' Dubeyji said morosely.

Ram Pratap Narayan Dubey alias Dubey! Dubeyji was not new to the university. He had come to the law faculty after doing a three-year BA and two-year MA. So, everyone in the university, from the proctor to the doctor, knew him well. Because of his connections and good relations with the proctor, he was also known as Al Dubeira. He had been given this name because he supplied everyone with the latest university news. Dubeyji had one paralysed leg; but it was also his weapon. He often used it to skip classes but still get his attendance marked. He knew exactly how to portray himself as helpless and get his jobs done.

His claim to fame was that even professors called him 'Dubeyji'. If there was any news in the university, it came first to Dubeyji. He made that molehill into a mountain and spread it to everyone. When it turned out to be true, he said proudly, 'Look, look! I had told you so, hadn't I?' It pleased Dubeyji greatly to be called Al Dubeira. His news updates were definitely true, it's just that he exaggerated them to make them more dramatic.

Dubeyji's problem was his English. His vocabulary was limited, and he hardly conversed in Hindi. He usually managed with Bhojpuri. But when Bhojpuri was not enough, he opened his treasure chest of Hindi. Someone's father had told him that English was crucial to practising in the Supreme Court. So, Dubeyji left his Hindi section and came to the English section, and was to present that day.

'Yes, so Dubeyji. Today is your presentation, am I right?' Pande Sir rubbed his hands together.

'Yes, Sir.' Dubeyji started speaking in English.

'Okay then. Start,' Sir said.

'Sir, good morning. Your name is Ram Pratap Narayan Dubey.'

'Not your, Dubeyji. My . . . my name is . . . '

'Sorry, Sir,' Dubeyji said.

'My name is Ram Pratap Narayan Dubey, and your topic is . . . ' Dubeyji made the same mistake again.

'Not your, Dubeyji, my. My means belonging to me, all right? Okay? Now carry on.'

'My name is Ram Pratap Narayan Dubey. My topic is Section 124 A and you are sodomy.'

'What? What nonsense! 124A is about sedition, not sodomy! Didn't anyone tell you that?' Pande Sir said, looking at his watch.

'Sorry, Sir. My name is Ram . . . ' Dubeyji's record was still playing.

'Dubeyji, I'll tell you what. Please give your presentation in Hindi.' Pande Sir was annoyed.

'Why, Sir? I'm a student of the English section and I've prepared everything in English.' Dubeyji was hurt by Sir's words.

'You've prepared? Which book have you prepared from, Dubeyji?' Pande Sir asked, putting his hands behind his back.

'Paras Diwan.' Dubeyji's blurted out the first name that came to his mind.

'Paras Diwan? Since when has Paras Diwan started writing about IPC?'

'S.N. Mishra! S.N. Mishra!' Dubeyji exclaimed, hearing whispers from behind.

'Which colour is S.N. Mishra's book, Dubeyji?' Pande Sir was not in a mood to let him go.

'It's yellow,' Dubeyji said confidently.

'As far as I remember, only the 1997 edition of his book was yellow. After that, I can't think of any.' Even Pande Sir was enjoying himself now.

'That's the edition I have, Sir,' Dubeyji said, finding a way out.

'Dubeyji, have you seen my name anywhere in that book? In the introduction, the preface or anywhere else?'

Dubeyji stopped for a minute, looked up and down and then asked, 'What is your name, Sir?'

Pande Sir was stunned. The classroom erupted into laughter. Pandeji ended the presentation.

* * *

The fourth-semester exams were about to begin. Usually, when everyone was busy with academics, a few people started thinking about attendance. Whether or not you scored 75 per cent, your attendance had to be 75 per cent. That is why all the preparations had been made in advance. Medical certificates had been provided, the attendance clerk had been spoken to but the attendance was still not enough. The least attendance was in Abhay Kumar's class. Therefore the holy gathering of the Mata was convened in front of his chamber.

'Who knows whether he'll give attendance?' Dada's asthma was increasing.

'If you're so scared, attend his classes!' Jaivardhan said, annoyed.

'Don't you wax eloquent in front of the chamber!' Dada said, taking a puff of his Asthalin inhaler.

'He'll give the attendance, man. The medical certificate is absolutely original this time. Don't you worry,' I said.

'Arre, Dubeyji, are you in line too?' Jaivardhan said.

'Haan, bhai. It's falling a little short, so I thought I'd meet him,' Dubeyji said, closing his umbrella.

'But Abhay Sir is often annoyed with you. Will he give you attendance?' I expressed my doubts.

'He definitely will. All of you may need to figure yours out, though.' Dubey had left us speechless. We were just discussing how many professors we would have to meet when Abhay Sir called out, 'What's up? Why are all of you standing here?'

'Good morning, Sir,' we chorused, entering the chamber.

'Yes, go on. Your presentation is still left, isn't it?' said Sir.

'No, Sir. We have made our presentations,' Jaivardhan said.

'Then?'

'Sir, attendance . . . ' I had just said this much when Sir interrupted me.

'Look, I don't want to be rude to you. Kindly leave before I say something.' Abhay Sir gestured towards the door.

'Sir, I was down with jaundice,' I said.

'What is your name?' asked Abhay Sir, pointing at me with a pencil.

'Sir . . . Suraj.'

'Suraj. You had got jaundice the last time as well,' he said, looking at his register.

'Yes, Sir.'

'And you had made this excuse in your first semester as well. As far as I know, a person can't have jaundice more than twice,' Abhay Sir said, drawing the number '2' in the air with his pencil.

'Sir, it was a hepatitis B issue this time. I was admitted as well. You can have a look at the medical certificate if you wish,' I said in one breath.

'No, no. There's no need for that. I have full faith in your attempts. Anyway, you are a hepatitis patient, you need prayers as well. I will not let your trust go in vain. Please go and prepare for the exams,' Abhay Sir sneered.

'Thanks, Sir.' His taunts didn't bother me, my job was done.

'Which illness were *you* suffering from, Dubeyji?' Abhay Sir turned towards Dubeyji.

'Sir, I am very poor and also paralysed. Your class is always after lunch. I walk to the hostel for lunch and return on foot. I am poor, so I cannot hire a rickshaw, and I am paralysed, so I cannot walk quickly. By the time I reach the faculty, your class has usually begun, and you always ask us not to enter the class when you are teaching. So, I don't enter. That's why my attendance is low.' Dubeyji started crying as he spoke without giving Abhay Sir a chance to interrupt.

Abhay Sir looked at Dubeyji for a while. He had nothing to say. When he did speak, it was just this: 'All right. I am marking you present this time, but next time I will make sure that my class is not right after lunch.'

'Sir, my name is Jaivardhan Sharma . . . ' Jaivardhan had only said this much when Abhay Sir fired up.

'You two! Leave at once! You spend all day taking your bike from Lanka to the faculty and from the faculty to Lanka. What do you do? Are you looking for passengers? You shameless people. At least you would have made some money if you had ferried people. Just leave right now!' said Abhay Sir, closing his file.

'Let's go, man. This guy's pissed,' Jaivardhan whispered, and we left the room.

'Look! This is called making an impression!' I teased.

'Yes, yes! Marry the girl who agrees with you, right?' Jaivardhan said softly.

'Go ahead, make your impression. We're going to Shrivastav Sir now, right? Let's see who makes an impression now!' Dada boasted.

Actually, Dada had helped Shrivastav Sir a lot. Once, when his mother was ill, Dada had taken her to the hospital on his bike and stayed with her there all night. That's why Shrivastav Sir trusted Dada.

'Good morning, Sir,' we chorused as we entered Shrivastav Sir's chamber. Dubeyji went a step ahead and touched his feet too.

'Oh, Anurag! Where were you? I didn't see you in class last month,' Shrivastav Sir asked, surprised.

'Sir, I was unwell,' Dada said, looking down.

'Oh. It's all right now, I hope. Go on, what brings you here today?'

'Sir, the attendance is falling a little short,' Dada said softly.

'Okay, I'll look into it. Just give me a medical certificate. Anything else?'

'Sir, it's the same case with me. Can I give a medical certificate too?' Jaivardhan did not want to lose the opportunity this time.

'Yes,' Shrivastav Sir said to Jaivardhan and looked at me.

'What is your problem?' he asked me.

'Sir, I was down with jaundice,' I repeated.

'So?' Sir asked shortly.

'So, Sir, my attendance fell short.'

'Fell short? Your attendance fell short? You proxy for the whole class. How can your attendance fall short?' Shrivastav Sir taunted.

'Sir, I had hepatitis B. You can see my medical certificate,' I said softly.

'If you can switch between three identities in a day, a medical certificate must be child's play for you. I cannot consider your application,' Shrivastav Sir said. Now I was speechless. Dada and Jaivardhan were smiling.

'Arre, Dubeyji! You're also in line? Haven't seen you in class for a while,' Shrivastav Sir turned to Dubeyji.

'No, Sir. I just came to seek blessings and offer prasad,' Dubeyji said confidently.

'What kind of prasad, Dubeyji?' asked Sir.

'Last year I went with my mother to offer prayers at the Kalighat temple. Actually, Kali Maa had appeared in my mother's dream and asked her to visit her shrine. Now, I have just one leg, so the two-day job ended up taking ten. I've just come from there. I've got some prasad for you too, Sir.' Dubeyji gave the prasad to Shrivastav Sir with his right hand.

'Oh, I see! That's why I haven't seen you around in class. Never mind. Everything will be all right with the blessings of Kali Maa. Go, prepare for your exams.' Shrivastav Sir touched the prasad to his forehead and wrapped it in some paper. We also left the room with Dubeyji.

'Lo beta! It's all even now. We didn't get attendance there, you didn't get it here,' Dada said.

'Yes. If even one is sorted, at least we'll be able to sit for the exams. But how did Dubey manage in both places?' I asked.

'Dubey, what was this prasad game, huh?' Jaivardhan asked.

'Nothing, what game would it be? As soon as I entered Shrivastav Sir's chamber, I saw there was a photo of Kali Maa, so I realized he's a devotee. So I made up a story!' Dubeyji.

'And prasad? What about the prasad? He's lying!' Dada said.

'What prasad? I was eating some puffed rice back at home; it was still in my pocket, so I took it out and gave it to him.' Dubeyji left us shocked as he calmly got a rickshaw and headed off.

* * *

'How was the paper?' Dada asked as we exited the exam hall.

'The Company Law paper was good, man,' I said.

'Where's Jaivardhan?' I asked, looking around.

'Inside. He's having a row with the invigilator about how he should get ten minutes more because the exam bell rang late,' Dada laughed.

'He's going to take a while; let's go get some tea in the canteen,' I said to Dada. There were already a few people when we got there. Just then, I spotted three empty chairs.

Dubeyji was sitting right next to them. We decided to sit there.

'*Aur*, Dubeyji? How was the paper?' I asked him as soon as I sat down.

'Kickass,' he replied.

'My paper wasn't good,' Dada said, sitting down.

'Why? Didn't you study Company Law in BCom as well?' I asked.

'That's why. I couldn't write all the types in the "types of shares" question. I remembered all, but there was no time,' Dada said, rubbing his hands.

'I just wrote what I remembered, man,' I said.

'Which question are you guys talking about?' Dubeyji asked, surprised.

'The fifth question, types of shares,' I said.

'Dude, Dubey will get confused. He writes papers in Hindi, tell him in Hindi,' Dada said.

'Oh, yes! Sorry, Dubeyji.' I translated it for him.

'They had asked for types of shares?' Dubeyji's face had gone pale.

'Yes, what did you think?' I asked.

'Goddamn it. No wonder I'm not getting marks. The question was types of shares, and I've written types of hares! How will I get marks?' Dubeyji said worriedly.

'What? Types of hares? My god, Dubey! Don't make us laugh. Come on, you fucker, get up from there.' Dada had fallen on the floor laughing.

'What are the types you have listed, Dubeyji?' I asked, suppressing my laughter.

'Scrub hare, mountain hare, cape hare . . . ' Dubeyji rattled off a whole list.

'Send him off, send this guy off!' Dada was rolling on the floor in a fit of laughter. He had forgotten that he was in the canteen.

'You're a suicide bomber, my friend! Look, Dada is dying of laughter there! Anyway, forget that, give us some new updates,' I said, trying not to laugh.

'You got into a fight at Lanka, didn't you?' Dubey said suddenly.

'How do you know?' My smile vanished.

'The proctor Tiwari was telling me, and he was asking about you as well,' Dubey said.

'What else was he saying?' I asked.

'He was saying something big is going to happen. But even he doesn't know what it is,' Dubey said, finishing his tea.

Lagaan: The Gentleman's Game

As a result of my dates with Shikha, my evenings were often spent in Assi Ghat, Madhuvan or in some restaurant. So, I wasn't able to give enough time to my friends. Dada and Jaivardhan realized this, but they were also worried about projects, which all three of us always borrowed from Shikha, so they never complained. Yes, they often jokingly quoted songs like '*dost dost na raha*' and said that their friend was not their friend any more. On an evening just like this, when I returned from meeting Shikha, Jaivardhan was sitting with his head in his hands.

'Why do you look upset, man?' I asked Jaivardhan.

'Jaivardhan Bhai is stressed,' said Dada, reading *Sports Star*.

'What happened? Is everything all right? The results aren't out, right?' I asked, getting upset.

'Ask the man himself,' Dada said.

'What happened, bey?' I asked.

'It's all because of you guys!' Jaivardhan was annoyed.

'Will you just tell us what happened?' I also asked angrily.

'I'll tell you,' Dada said. 'When we were going to class yesterday, our man was playing cricket with the seniors here. He got out on a duck, got infuriated and challenged the seniors to a cricket match.'

'That idiot threw a random spinning ball anywhere and said LBW! You tell me, can you even have an LBW in the hostel?'

'So, dude, why do you always fly into a temper?' I scolded.

'So, what should I fly into, then? Ghanta? The juniors say I can't do anything except chase girls on my bike. It's all because of you!' Jaivardhan tried to make himself feel better.

'Is that so?' I asked.

'No, no, I'm a freaking madman sitting here making up stories. Babuji is right, keep good company and there's a lot to get, keep bad company and you'll be injured to death,' Jaivardhan said, upset.

'Well done, raja. There's nothing greater than honour. We have to show them all,' Dada said, taking Jaivardhan's side.

'Ghanta! Don't you keep saying raja-raja, it's like the lead actress of *Mastram* is calling me. My mood is not great right now anyway!'

'And who said the thing about going after girls?' I asked.

'You shut up, man. Just poke your nose whenever anyone talks about girls. Think about cricket. Now that it's settled, it's settled,' Dada said.

'That's your job, you do the thinking," I said, snatching the *Sports Star*.

'When's the match?' Dada asked.

'Sunday,' Jaivardhan said, getting up.

* * *

Cricket was played every evening in Bhagwandas Hostel, where seniors and juniors all got together. But several people did not like playing against the seniors in fields outside Bhagwandas. They had several reasons. One was to stay in the seniors' good books so they could get help with placements later. Another was the fear of playing in front of Murali Sir, lest he assume that these people were not serious about their studies. Also, there was the anxiety of not being able to submit projects and presentations on time.

Because of all these fears, tears, so's and though's, it was difficult to gather a team of eleven players, but, ultimately, we did convince the adequate number.

Dada
Suraj, that is, me
Amit
Nirbhay
Gunjan
Jaivardhan
Navendu
Kamlesh

Kaunjum

Ashish

And Vineet

A total of 11!

If there was anything Dada took seriously in life, it was cricket. I had realized this in all these days of living with him. He never watched cricket in the common room. This was because he disapproved of any kind of joking around when he was watching the game. He was extremely passionate about it hence the most worried about the match—even more than Jaivardhan. He hadn't slept well the previous night. The next morning, when I saw him strolling aimlessly in the room, I brought him to Assi Ghat. Assi Ghat—the ghat of the unexplainably distressed souls.

'Bhaiya, two cups of tea,' Dada said.

'Ask for snacks also,' I teased Dada. I often said this when I wanted to lighten the mood. But today, Dada did not react.

'Who'll be the umpire, man?' Dada said, ignoring me.

'Murali Sir and one of the hostel staff.'

'No wonder the seniors were following Murali Sir around all of yesterday,' Dada said, picking up the cups of tea.

'So what?' I asked, taking one from Dada.

'Dude, the seniors will make life hell for us if we lose! They've been taunting us since yesterday that we have chosen a team from all over India. Plus, we don't even have a game plan,' Dada said, putting his head in his hands.

'What do we need a game plan for? We'll just go and play,' I said, taking a sip.

'Yes, and then we'll lose. Each player is one of a kind! One calls LBW LPW. You don't know the difference between long on and long off. All of these are rough players. What if they start fighting physically after getting out? Plus, you've made me the captain.' Dada was extremely worried.

'Don't worry, our team will wi . . . look! Shikha!' I said, looking down.

'Now you'll make Shikha play cricket? How did Shikha come into cricket?' Dada asked, annoyed.

'Look down. She's having chaat at the Bhaukal chaat counter.'

'Go, raja! My destiny dictates that I must make the plan myself!' laughed Dada.

'No, man. Ever since the fight at Lanka, she doesn't want to talk outside the faculty, and even I avoid it.'

'The point is, you two aren't able to exchange sweet nothings. Look there! Mr Jaivardhan is also coming!' Dada said. Jaivardhan was parking a cycle at the stand. He had borrowed it. If Jaivardhan had borrowed a cycle and brought it to Assi Ghat, then something was definitely wrong. If everything had been all right, Jaivardhan would have waited for us to return to the hostel.

'What're you doing here, man?' Dada asked Jaivardhan the moment he arrived.

'Dude, everything's going wrong there and you're here playing games like lover boys? Ah, says my restless heart, upset as it cannot stay apart. One eats chaat, while the other drools from his mouth!' Jaivardhan said in a single breath.

'Cut the babble and tell me, what's wrong?' I asked.

'Dada, get me some chaat first, please!' Jaivardhan said.

'Come, I'll get it today,' I said.

'Bhaukal bhai, three plates of chaat, please,' Dada said as we reached the chaat counter.

'And take the money for five plates.' Jaivardhan had counted Shikha and her friend as well.

'Abey, won't you tell us what's wrong?' Dada asked.

'Ashish Rai has refused to play,' Jaivardhan said.

'Why?' I asked, looking at Shikha.

'He says, exams are coming. He's promised his father he won't come home without a gold medal, so he needs to study for that,' Jaivardhan said, swallowing a spoonful.

'Even I've promised my mother that I won't show her my face till I bring her daughter-in-law home,' I said, without lifting my eyes from Shikha.

'So come on, get married right here! The pandit is here, so are the *baraatis*!' Jaivardhan joked.

'The bride's not ready, bro,' I said, gesturing towards Shikha, who had started to leave.

'*Bakaiti band kar*. Cut the crap and think, what do we do now?' Dada said.

'Here my heart is so lost it needs a map and you're talking about crap?' I said, finishing the chaat.

'If you guys won't laugh, there is a solution,' Jaivardhan said.

'Go on, raja!' I said as I watched Shikha disappear into the distance. I still hoped she would turn back to look at me.

'Moos! Our mess boy! Let's take him.'

'Moos . . . dude, how will Moos play?' Dada asked, surprised.

'And how do you think Navendu will play? We just need to reach the eleven mark, and anyway, when the ten of us can't get anything done then it is unfair to expect something from the eleventh,' Jaivardhan said.

'What do you say, Suraj?' Dada asked me.

'Take anyone, man! Here my family is crumbling. The girl just paid for the chaat and left!' I said, upset.

'Just go die for the girl! On one side there's the girl who didn't even look up once, and here's Mr Dev Anand, who looks as if he will drown in her eyes and never wake up!' Jaivardhan said angrily.

'No, no, we're all listening, man. Yes, Moos will play!' I sealed the deal.

* * *

Tens of papers were covered in plans in the lead-up to Sunday. A field setting was designed. The papers were torn up. There were fights on who would bat first. The fights were resolved. Then, at last, Sunday arrived. Murali Sir, who was serving the dual role of the umpire and the match referee, started explaining the rules.

'Both teams must be listening carefully. There is being no sledging in the match. Juniors are to being respecting the seniors. The match is for twenty-twenty overs. One player be doing four overs. After result, the seniors be offering breakfast to the juniors. If there are any questions, they will be asked right now.'

'No, Sir. Shall we go for the toss?' Dada asked.

'Yes, both captains be coming forward,' Murali Sir said, taking a step ahead.

'Dada, take this coin with you. It's lucky for me. Always lands on tails, say tails,' Jaivardhan said.

'Here, give it to me.' Dada took the coin and went for the toss.

'I've given Dada the coin. Bhole Baba will help us win the toss,' Jaivardhan said.

'Who's the captain from that side?' I asked.

'Smart Nishant,' Jaivardhan replied.

'Smart Nishant. Is that his name?' Jaivardhan asked.

'I don't know, it's what his batchmates call him,' I said.

'It's important to know the names. There'll be no fun without that,' Vineet said.

'But sledging is against the rules.' I had understood what Vineet meant.

'Oh, a lot of things are against the rules! The rules can't spoil the fun,' Vineet said, rubbing his eyes.

'Dada is coming, it seems the toss is over. What happened, boy?' I asked.

'We won the toss. I've chosen to field,' Dada said, throwing the ball into the air.

'What! You ass, who chooses to field after winning the toss?' Jaivardhan said angrily.

'There's dew on the pitch. Bowling first will help,' Dada explained.

'Ghanta it will help! This is Birla Hostel's field, not the Mohali Stadium!' Jaivardhan was sounding really low.

'Aditya Pancholi made a similar mistake in the movie *Awwal Number*, because of which . . . ' Navenduji said when Jaivardhan interrupted him.

'Yes, Navenduji. We know your bones are ancient, you have even witnessed the childhood of A.K. Hangal. Come, let's get this fish! Let's go field,' Jaivardhan said, getting up.

Dada had set the field according to his plan, in which I had been positioned at third man. Before the match started, I asked Dada, 'Who's going for the first over?'

'Nirbhay.'

'Nirbhay! Why are you giving Nirbhay the ball, huh? Virendar Rai is coming out to bat, he'll destroy the field!'

'His length is good. Virender and Nishant Bhaiya will both have issues,' Dada said, throwing the ball to Nirbhay. I returned to third man. The game was just about to commence. All fielders were ready at their positions.

Nirbhay was ready at the run-up with the ball. Murali Sir signalled for the match to begin. Nirbhay bowled the first ball fast, and Nishant Sir hit it outside the boundary line even faster.

'There you go! Smart Nishant hit an effing boundary on the first ball! Never mind, let's say c'mon, c'mon a couple of times, everything will be all right,' Jaivardhan said.

'Never mind, Nirbhay! It was an unplanned shot, keep going!' Dada shouted.

'It was the first four of his life, he won't hit another one!' Jaivardhan also shouted.

'Bring Suraj here from third man, it's not fun otherwise,' Jaivardhan said in the middle of the over.

'Is he here for you to have fun on the field? Just shut up and field,' Dada scolded.

'Dude! Why is this Smart Nishant wearing glasses, huh?' Jaivardhan asked.

'He thinks his girlfriend could show up to watch the match anytime, so he's prepared,' Dada said.

'Even Smart Nishant has a girlfriend! We're the only unlucky ones,' Jaivardhan said, throwing the ball to Nirbhay.

I was given the second over. I conceded a total of seven runs. Virender Rai even hit a four at mid-on, but I managed my over. Even then, the score was more than we expected, also because the seniors did not play too well in the small ground inside the hostel. This mindset was our mistake. They had scored twenty-seven runs in just three overs.

'Dude, Smart Nishant is hitting the ball all over the park! They've made twenty-seven runs in three overs, what do we do?' Dada asked me.

'Okay, look. Moos has a voice like a girl's. Tell him to call our hostel and say that he's Shivani, and to call Nishant from room number 18,' I said, rubbing the ball.

'How will that help?' Dada asked, taking the ball from me and cleaning it with his hand.

'Shivani is Smart Nishant's girlfriend's and he never misses a single phone call from her. He pays the hostel peon 100 rupees and has told him that he should never miss a single phone call. When Shivani calls, the peon will definitely come from the hostel and tell Smart Nishant, and then, I bet, Smart Nishant will ditch the pitch and leave,' I said, handing the ball to Nirbhay.

Dada immediately explained this to Moos and handed him his phone. Moos repeated what he had memorized. Within ten minutes, the Bhagwandas peon Laalji came running.

'Nishant Bhaiya, there is phone call for you. From where you know! Very urgent!' Lalji said, panting.

Needless to say that Smart Nishant was dismissed and was standing at the girls' hostel gate within ten minutes.

But Virender Rai took on the responsibility to finish Smart Nishant's incomplete task. All the pitch reports and dew reports seemed to fail when fifty-six runs were made in seven overs. Afridi had come alive in Virender Rai. That day, we saw all kinds of non-cricketing shots, like the reverse pull and the reverse hook. After I was hit for twenty runs in one over, they did not take the risk of giving me the ball again. Virender Rai was not in the mood to spare anyone. That's when a miracle happened.

'Buffalo shot!' came Vineet's voice from behind the wicket.

Actually, Vineet and Virender were classmates in school and since then Vineet used to tease him with this name, but now Virender Rai was his senior and he found it humiliating. Virender got very angry, but kept his cool and left the next ball for the wicketkeeper.

'Buffalo left!' called the voice again.

This baffled Virender, and he had decided to hit the wicketkeeper with the next ball, so he stood very close to the wicket. But as soon as he lifted his bat to hit the next ball, the bat hit the wicket and Virender Rai was dismissed hit wicket. He left, showing the wicketkeeper, Vineet, his bat. Our job was done and so was Virender Rai's. By the time he was dismissed, the score was ninety-six in twelve overs. Murali Sir announced a break.

'My friend, the seniors will start a ragging session part 2 for us after we reach the hostel, be prepared!' Jaivardhan said, splashing water on his head.

'Abey, forget about that. Tell me, what do we do now? No bowler seems to be working out,' Dada said, taking the water bottle from him.

'Try my leg spin also, I throw just like Abdul Qadir!' Navenduji said.

'Oh, so that means you spin more than the ball does,' Jaivardhan said hotly.

'Everyone's being hit over the park. Go, Navenduji, you bowl,' Dada said, throwing the ball his way.

'Yes, give it to him. A little token for a tiny sick lamb! But be careful, don't jump around too much or you'll dislocate a bone, and bones at this age . . . I'm sure you know,' Jaivardhan teased.

Jaivardhan would often say that coins we deem useless used to be ducats in their day. Today was Navenduji's day and he truly was a golden coin in his day. Navenduji's bowling figure after the match was something like this.

Three overs-one maiden-four wickets.

Navenduji's googly, backhand, fronthand, *doosra*, *teesra*, slipper, flipper, mystery ball, history ball, back-of-the-hand ball, all mystified the seniors. The team could only make 123 runs. Murali Sir gave a fifteen-minute break. Everyone, even the seniors, was praising Navenduji's bowling. Navenduji himself was proud of his performance.

'Did you see my leg spin! It was leaning to the right and speeding towards the left!' Navenduji said, sitting down.

'Yes, Navenduji. Just like your rickshaw sped towards the left and you fell into a drain after seating us in it!' I revealed a secret.

'Oh, no. That day the front wheel slipped on a banana peel.' Navenduji saved his face.

'Navenduji, you can drive rickshaws too?' Vineet asked.

'There you go! Don't you know this? There's not a thing Navenduji can't do! He's even returned from the dead twice!' Jaivardhan did not want to miss a single opportunity to teasing him.

'Guys, stop this chatter now. Who's going to open? We need to score with an average of six.' Dada said.

'I will. Because we need a fast start,' I said.

'I will. I won't let my wicket fall,' Gunjan contested.

'What's the argument? I will open. You people, ghanta gave me a chance to bowl,' Jaivardhan said, practising his batting.

'Bhaiya, I go into the field?' Moos was not inferior to anyone.

'I couldn't do anything great with the ball, but I will with the bat,' Nirbhay said.

'The batting won't be affected if I get out, so let me go,' was Navenduji's statement.

'I hit thunderous shots, *ekdum bumpilaat*!' Amit offered.

'*Jhampo Telam ki Jai*!' Kaunjum Tasho knew only one line in Hindi which he continuously threw at us.

'Nobody's going! I will go and Vineet will go with me.' Dada made the final decision.

'Idiot's taken it too seriously because he's the captain. When I'm captain in the next match, I'll bowl all twenty overs and I'll bat all twenty too, with Moos,' Jaivardhan said, putting the bat down.

It was truly a difficult task to open. All eleven players wanted to bat first, and it was very tough to refuse anyone. After all, they were all friends. This argument about who should open was going on when Dubeyji entered and immediately solved the problem.

'Nishant Sir has arrived, and news has reached the girls' hostel that seniors have beaten the juniors. Meenakshi Ma'am has told our batchmates that the juniors are all useless.' Dubeyji gave us the breaking news as soon as he came.

'Damn it! It's a matter of honour now! Dada and Vineet, you two go bat and someone beat that Dubey up! Asshole never comes with good news,' I said, handing Vineet the bat.

'Here, hold my phone and sweater. I'll return victorious,' Dada said confidently and approached the field. In a while,

Dada and Vineet were both in the crease and playing carefully.

'Oh, look! Smart Nishant is bowling with glasses on!' I said.

'Why are you so keen on his glasses, dude?' Jaivardhan said.

'Look carefully. Either he doesn't know they're ladies' goggles or he's borrowed them from his girlfriend to show off,' I said.

'What a boy, my oxygen! You could score enough to be the next Jethmalani if you concentrated so much on your studies.'

'It's runs that are being scored as of now. Dada and Vineet are batting well. Dude, what does Smart Nishant's girlfriend look like?' I asked.

'I don't know and don't disturb me. Can't you see I'm writing the score? Ask Navenduji, he knows everything.'

'Navenduji, what does Nishant Sir's girlfriend look like?' I asked.

'She's our senior. We shouldn't talk about her like this.' Navenduji was a saintly man.

'Arre, it's not like I've asked you her measurements! If I spot her in the faculty sometime, how will I give her respect her if I don't recognize her?' I gave a valid reason.

'You are right. If unknowingly something goes wrong then . . . '

'And Vineet hit a four!'

'Good job, Babu Sahib!'

'Take their ghanta and hit it hard!'

'Come on, kill them!' Jaivardhan was out of control.

Vineet had hit a four and here Navenduji was hitting sixes with his descriptions of beauty.

'Her complexion is as if someone has mixed a dollop of crimson into pure white butter.' Navenduji started explaining.

'Navenduji reads a lot of Reema Bharti stories. That's where he's got this line,' I laughed.

'Reema Bharti reminds me, exams are coming. Collect her books, they're necessary to be able to stay up all night. What a mystery we had found in the last book, we were hungover on it for a week!' Jaivardhan said, writing down runs.

'You guys keep changing the topic! Yes, Navenduji, she is very fair, but there could be four dozen fair women in the faculty. How will I recognize her?' I asked.

'Are they women or bananas, you ass, counting them in dozens. Look there, Smart Nishant is delivering bouncers to Dada and the umpire isn't even signalling a no-ball!' Jaivardhan was getting upset.

'Yes, so Navenduji. You were giving some details about Shivaniji.' I started the story again.

'My god, just tell this idiot please else he's going to get struck by lightning right here, isn't he?' Jaivardhan fumed.

'Shivani Ma'am has studied in a convent, and Nishant Sir was telling me that she'll do an LLM from London after finishing her LLB here,' Navenduji kept up the conversation.

'Yes, of course she'll do it in London . . . look there! Now what is Rajesh Bhaiya telling Dada?' Jaivardhan was concentrating both on and off the field.

'There's some sledging going on. Dada will handle it. How many runs?' I asked.

'It's forty-one runs in six overs. Now we have to make eighty-four runs in eighty-three balls. We'll have to keep playing at this rate to win,' Jaivardhan said.

'Oh . . . n . . . oo! Vineet got out! Vineet really got out!' Jaivardhan was unable to believe it. Vineet got greedy when he saw Krishnan Sir's flight and got stumped in his rush to get ahead and hit the ball.

'Jaivardhan, you go and tell Dada he can rest if he's tired. I'll speak to Murali Sir,' I said, giving Jaivardhan the bat. Jaivardhan immediately put on his pads and entered the field. Vineet had also come by then.

'Dada isn't able to run,' Vineet said, taking off his gloves.

'Sit down, Babu Sahib. If you hadn't been dismissed you would have returned only after playing the twentieth over today,' I said.

'Twentieth? Oh no, I would have finished the game in the sixteenth over,' Vineet said, taking off his pads.

'Jaivardhan also plays well. Let's see how he does today,' I said, noting down the runs.

'Dada isn't able to run. The run rate will fall, we'll have to keep taking singles,' Dubeyji, who had been silent so far, said. I forgot all my worries the moment I heard Dubeyji's voice. Now I started thirsting for some spicy gossip.

'Don't worry, Dubeyji, Dada will handle it. You give us some news,' I said, sitting down next to him.

'A CD has been seized from the girls' hostel.' Dubeyji immediately provided some spicy news.

'Fucker, you're lying. I met the proctor Tiwary only today. He didn't mention anything like this,' Vineet egged Dubey on.

'Hey, let me complete. The CD had the Durga Chalisa, Sai Chalisa and the Satya Narayan Katha on it. All religious material.' Dubeyji changed the topic immediately. The game was also changing.

'Look at that! Jaivardhan got run-out and now he's arguing with Murali Sir! Send Kamlesh,' I said. Kamlesh was ready with his pad and gloves, and stepped into the field. Jaivardhan was returning, thumping his bat.

'What's up, dude? What were you arguing with Murali Sir about?' Vineet asked Jaivardhan the moment he returned.

'Man! I wasn't out. I had reached, but was dismissed because of pressure from the seniors.' Jaivardhan was angry.

'You seemed out from this angle,' Vineet said.

'No, man! I had definitely reached. I haven't given his presentation, that's why he dismissed me,' Jaivardhan said, taking a seat.

'Shut up, dude! First you say it was because of the seniors, then you say it was because of the presentation. You were out,' I said. Jaivardhan was presenting his testimony here, and there, the game was still on.

Because of the good partnership between Dada and Kamlesh, sixty-three runs had been scored in nine overs so far. Now there were sixty-six runs required in sixty balls. Dada and Kamlesh were playing carefully and taking most runs as singles and doubles. The game was getting a little boring because of the lack of fours and sixes. In this situation, I thought of Dubeyji once more. I asked him for more news. His Al Dubeira channel started promptly. Some of the main news pieces were:

- The criminology paper will get leaked this time.
- A whole basket of condoms has been found in the IT hostel.
- Nobody has ever seen Falaana Sir take a shower.
- Roshan Chaudhuri works in a garage at night.
- Amitabh Bachchan has lost his hair. He wears a wig now.

Before Dubeyji could give more news, the match had reached an interesting point and nobody wanted to listen him anymore. Dada was finding it difficult to run, so only thirty-two runs were scored off the next eight overs. Now we needed twenty-eight runs in three overs to win.

'It's Ranjan Bhaiya's last over. They should take a chance in this one,' I said.

'Yes, they have to start hitting now. We need to pluck the mangoes even if we lose the stick,' Jaivardhan said.

'Kamlesh is doing well. He's taking singles and giving Dada the strike,' Navenduji said.

'We'll win, man,' I said.

'Dada's hit it hard! And it goes . . . goes . . .goes . . . four!' Jaivardhan had a style of his own.

'Attaboy! That's a shot!' Even I shouted.

'What's the score?' Navenduji asked.

'We need nineteen runs in fifteen balls now,' Vineet said.

'Six . . . Oh . . . Dude, it got caught! Shit, yaar! Dude, Dada got out! Dada shouldn't have got out at this point,' I said, holding my head.

'Yes, it was time to finish the game now!' Vineet said.

'Send Navenduji,' Jaivardhan said.

'Kamlesh will have to handle everything now,' Dada said as he returned. But Dada did not take long to come back and neither did Navenduji.

'Good god! Navenduji got smashed in the first ball itself! The ball slipped between his feet, he got bowled! Who sent him, huh? Paint my freaking fart, what is this ass dandruff! Created pressure for nothing!' Jaivardhan said.

'Let me go,' I said.

'Yes, go, and don't let it be a hattrick or Ranjan Bhaiya won't let me live,' Dada said to me.

'Come, Navenduji, sit. You took enough trouble, you may surrender now,' Jaivardhan said to Navenduji, who was just returning.

I had just reached the crease. I took an off-stump guard and waited for Ranjan Bhaiya's ball; I thought he would bowl a yorker. But contrary to my expectations, he bowled a short ball, and contrary to my luck, the ball did not come up to my bat. It trailed the ground and hit my middle stump. I was left staring at the pitch. Murali Sir lifted his forefinger.

'Oh, no! Suraj also got bowled. What did the fucker even go to do?' Dada said.

'Look at Ranjan Bhaiya! He looks like he's dancing at a wedding!' Vineet said.

'Of course he will, he just took a hattrick,' Dada replied.

'You're just capable of writing runs, you idiot. You can't hit a single ball! Only in a world of ghanta will we win now!' Jaivardhan said as I arrived.

'What's the score?' I asked.

'It's the same score that you left behind. The game is over.'

'What are you asking the score for? We need nineteen runs in two overs. Put so much pressure on Kamlesh,' Dada said. The game had suddenly slipped out of our hands. The victory, which appeared so easy in Kamlesh and Dada's presence, was moving away from us just in the last three balls.

'Let's call a few boys from outside, they'll come and break the game. Our honour will be saved,' Vineet suggested.

'No, man. What is to happen will happen on the field now,' I said.

'Nirbhay has gone. Let's see what he does,' Dada replied.

'Sanjeev Bhaiya will bowl the nineteenth over and the last one will definitely be by Smart Nishant,' I said.

The match had reached a nail-biting point. A point at which being a senior or a junior did not mean anything. A point at which our professor's presence did not mean anything. If there was anything that had meaning, it was just the two overs that were to come and the nineteen runs that could or could not be scored. Victory could swing either way. Amid this pressure, stress and uncertainty, Sanjeev Sir bowled his first ball to Nirbhay.

'Six . . .! *Hurr hurrr hurr*! Hit it on his first ball . . . hurr hurr hurrr!'

'Go, Nirbhay! One more, we want one more!' Vineet shouted.

'He's taken one run. That's okay. Kamlesh will play now.'

'And he hit it hard . . . going . . . going . . . going . . . going . . . gone! He raised his bat and put up a fight, here take some sugar next bite!' Jaivardhan's idioms were beyond our understanding.

'Now we need six runs in nine balls. That will be easy,' I said.

'Oh, he's hit it hard . . .! Another six . . . Kamlesh has hit it!'

Hurr hurr hurr hurr.

Game over.

Hurr hurr hurr hurr.

The game was over. The nineteen runs for which we had waited with bated breath had been scored in just four balls. Jaivardhan ran to lift the wicket, Dada ran to meet Murali Sir, and I started to call Shikha to inform her of the victory. The others were meeting the seniors, drinking tea and praising Murali Sir's umpiring. Murali Sir, like always, was giving the seniors career tips and advising them to study. After the conversations and breakfast were over, our team returned to the hostel.

'Now I feel like a real person!' Dada said, crashing on his bed.

'Yes, man, winning has a high of its own, don't you think?'

'Yeah, man, but you had made all the preparations to lose! Got out on a duck, three wickets in that over. That's when everything went wrong,' Dada said, covering his eyes with the blanket.

'Man, I couldn't understand the ball, but I'm the one who fixed everything. If I hadn't got Moos to make that phone call then the score would have been something else entirely.'

'Phone? Dude, where's my phone?' Dada asked, hurriedly throwing his blanket.

'Arre, yaar!' Even I got worried. The win had got me so excited that I had forgotten to take care of the phone. Dada had given me both his sweater and phone while going in to bat.

'Did you bring it or not?'

'Yes, man. I brought it from the field. I entered the hostel, then kept your sweater and phone, and started drinking water. I don't remember what happened after that,' I said, checking my pockets.

'Call it, quick!' Dada, but snatched my phone and started dialling quickly.

'What's it saying?' I asked, upset.

'The number you are trying to reach is switched off," Dada said, disconnecting the call.

'Oh, no. I think someone made off with it,' I said softly.

'Hmm . . . ' Dada replied.

'Or maybe the battery ran out?' I said, thinking.

'Maybe, but one thing is for certain. The phone's not coming back. Come, let's report it at the police station,' Dada said.

'Now let it go. Where will you go running after the police? The phone's not coming back.'

'It can be misused, man,' Dada said.

'Ghanta it'll get misused. My ID card got lost, did anything happen? Let it go,' I said to Dada.

'I would have let it go if the phone were in my name. But the phone is in my mother's name, so I will file a report.' Dada started his bike and left.

Kohraam: Chaos

The fifth-semester results were out. Almost everyone was making plans for their future. Shikha had an aggregate of 71 per cent. She was interested in academics, so she wanted an LLM. Law was Dada's family's profession, so he was not worried either. Jaivardhan had applied to a big Delhi law firm, Mehra and Mehra, for an internship and received a call. All he was waiting for was his final results. If they were worried about anyone, it was me. What would become of me? My marks were all right, but I did not want to study further, and there was no lawyer in my family whose position I could take over. I had given a few interviews, the results of which I was awaiting. I was always hopeful of interview results. What I didn't know was that destiny was planning something different for us. Something very, very dangerous.

Time: 8:35 a.m.

'Where's Navenduji? I haven't seen him in a while?' I asked Dada, who was brushing his teeth.

'Saw him just this morning; he's going to Patna today. He was saying that his uncle from Patna is ill,' laughed Dada.

'He and his uncles! Name one district where he doesn't have an uncle!' Even I was laughing.

'Come, let's go meet him. Let's catch up,' I said, getting up.

* * *

Time: 8:55 a.m.

When we went to Navenduji's room, we found out he was in the mess. While proceeding towards the mess, we ran into Jaivardhan. We spotted Navenduji sitting at a table just as we entered the mess. Jaivardhan went straight towards the food.

'Hey, what's there for lunch?' I asked the cook.

'Roti, dal and jackfruit koftas,' he said respectfully.

'Please bring them. I'm very hungry today, and then we have to go to class as well,' I said.

'I don't eat jackfruit,' Jaivardhan said, looking at the koftas.

'Just eat what is there, we have to go to class,' I said.

'Navenduji, are you getting a first division in your cumulative scores so far?' I asked.

'Yes, 67 per cent,' Navenduji said.

'Why won't he get a first division? Projects, presentations, everything on time. Says Yes Sir, No Sir to the lecturer, everything on time. Lecturer's fruit, vegetables, grocery shopping, everything on time. The cow gives milk and gets the grain!' Jaivardhan said, sorting out the koftas and keeping them aside.

'Is it wrong to submit projects and presentations on time? Is it wrong to respect elders? And marks show your hard work. Is it wrong to score marks? Come on, eat quickly. It's time for Abhay Kumar's lecture,' Navenduji said, washing his hands.

Time: 5:30 p.m.

There was barely time to even breathe after entering class. The lecturers were all in a hurry to complete the syllabi, so no class was ever cancelled. Classes in the last semester had suddenly become boring because anxiety about the future had set in. The ones who wanted to practise law had started looking for internships under good senior advocates. The ones who wanted to pursue advanced study had started preparing for LLM already.

'Dude, three back-to-back classes are exhausting! Let's go to the canteen and get some tea,' Dada said.

'No, let's go to the hostel, we'll get tea there,' I said.

'You guys go. I will go to Sankat Mochan Temple today. Ma was saying, who could be a greater sinner than you? People from all over the world go to Banaras to visit the temple, and you stay there and haven't gone even once,' Jaivardhan said.

'Get some prasad for us as well! And don't you snatch it from a monkey!' shouted Dada, and turned the key in his bike.

'This is the first time Jaivardhan has said no for tea. I don't think everything is quite all right,' I said, sitting behind Dada on the bike.

'Were you watching *The Sixth Sense* last night? Don't look for ghosts in tea at least! By the time we reach the hostel and get tea, Jaivardhan will also join us,' Dada said, and we took off.

Time: 6:00 p.m.

Just as I reached the hostel, I saw Navenduji leaving with a bag on his shoulders. A rickshaw was waiting for him outside. Now that we had made eye contact, I asked idly, 'Navenduji, when will you return?'

'I'll come as soon as Uncle is better!' Navenduji said, getting into a rickshaw.

'All right, then! Happy journey!' I waved.

Dada opened a packet of biscuits as we entered our room. I changed my clothes and picked up a biscuit. Today I didn't even feel like watching a movie on my laptop; I was in a state of confusion.

'Want to play cricket?' Dada asked.

'No, come, let's play volleyball,' I said.

'Jiyo Raja! Come,' Dada taunted.

'I'll serve,' I said, joining a volleyball team.

'All right, serve. I'll watch your game today.' Dada came and stood right behind me.

'Here goes my serve!' I said.

Time: 6:20 p.m.

Disaster issues its warnings before it strikes. The mind becomes doubtful. The heart starts beating faster for no good reason. You start behaving in an unusual manner. That day, I had decided to play volleyball to distract myself even though I didn't even know how much a volleyball weighed before this. I started feeling uneasy the moment Jaivardhan left for the temple. I could not tell Dada this. I was getting a premonition once more.

'Careful, dude!' Dada said, pulling at my arm.

A dry branch from a supari tree had come crashing down on my head. There were supari trees all around the hostel whose branches often dried up and fell, but the tremor this was caused was unusual and so was the sound that accompanied it.

'Dude, where did that sound come from?'

'There must have been a bomb blast somewhere,' Dada joked.

'But this dry branch fell because of that sound.'

'Not just this one. Dry branches from the other trees also fell because of the same sound,' Dada said, looking around.

'I hope there hasn't been an air crash somewhere?'

'The airport is far from the city and there's no aviation base here, so don't think too much and play volleyball.'

'Wait a minute, Shikha's calling. I'll talk to her, you play for me,' I said to Dada.

'Hello. Yes? Yes, even I heard the sound. No, nothing like that. Yeah man, I'm in the hostel. No, I'm not outside. Okay, bye.'

Time: 6:40 p.m.

Jaivardhan was still not back and the volleyball game was also over. Dada and I had just freshened up and left for tea when we saw Navenduji getting down from a rickshaw. I was surprised to see him return. I was just about to ask him why when Dada said, 'Navenduji, you're back? Your uncle kicked the bucket already, huh?'

'Dude, wish well for someone at least! There's been blasts in the Sankat Mochan and Cantt Station areas. They're not letting anyone go beyond Ravidas Gate. I heard seven people have been killed. There's nobody there from our hostel, right?'

'Jaivardhan!' Dada and I yelled simultaneously.

'Dada! Get the bike out, quick!' I shouted.

Time: 6:55 p.m.

Sankat Mochan had been transformed into a shelter. The temple premises were closed and people were being prevented from entering it. The unconscious were being brought out and sent to the nearby Sir Sunderlal Hospital. The news of the blast had spread like wildfire. The whole city was in shock. Most people had been wounded in the chaos after the blast. The injured were mostly women and old people. Attempts to avoid the stampede had caused accidents. I wanted to inform my family that I was all right; they would have heard the news. I tried to call, but it did not go through. Even Jaivardhan was not visible anywhere.

'They're not letting anyone go beyond the barricade, and Jaivardhan didn't even have a phone,' I said.

'The wounded are all around, where do we look for him?' Dada asked.

'Come, let's look among the wounded.'

'Why among the wounded? Why among the wounded? He's just fine. Nothing can happen to him.' The situation had put Dada in a shock.

'What kind of shirt was Jaivardhan wearing?' I asked.

'Was? What do you mean was? Ask, what shirt is Jaivardhan wearing today? Nothing has happened to him, do you understand?' Dada's voice was getting hoarse.

'Listen, Dada, I understand your condition. I feel the same way. But think about it, if he's wounded and needs our help, and if we can't reach on time despite being here, then we'll regret it our whole life. That's why I'm asking, what was the colour of his shirt?' I explained to Dada.

'White,' Dada said, dabbing the corners of his eyes with his thumb.

'All right, you wait here. I'll go take a look,' I said.

The bomb blast scene had been sealed. The ubiquitous monkeys had vanished. The delicate engravings in the courtyard had been stained red and the bloody footprints of the injured were still fresh. The sound of sirens was echoing. The police was having to persevere relentlessly to keep the public and press under control.

Dada was having a heated argument with the soldiers to be let in. My eyes were looking for a white shirt, but I could see none as blood had coloured some shirt collars and pockets, while others had been drenched entirely. When I tried to lift a man thinking he was Jaivardhan, his hand fell apart and came into mine. I jumped back. The man was dead. I wanted to scream, but it got stuck in my throat. The shouts, moans and groans of the wounded were testing my courage, but I still looked at almost all the wounded lying outside. Jaivardhan was not among them. For the first time I felt Jaivardhan may not have survived, but it was important for me to find him, no matter in what condition. I thought of looking among the dead in the hospital, but before I could reach any conclusion, Dada came running and placed his hand on my shoulder. When I looked back, there were tears in his eyes. He gestured at something and said, 'Look there. Jaivardhan is carrying someone on his shoulders. That is Jaivardhan, isn't it?'

'Yes, yes, it's him! Jaivardhan! Jaivardhan!' I shouted loudly and ran towards him.

'Abey, when did you guys come? Didn't you hear, there's been a bomb blast?' Jaivardhan said, placing the wounded man on a stretcher.

'No, no, how would we hear? We came here to party and we ran into you!' Dada said.

'All right, blabber later. Pick up this man now, he needs to be taken to the hospital. He has injuries on his leg and stomach,' Jaivardhan said.

* * *

Banaras—the land of moksha. Here, death means reaching nirvana and life means hedonism. It is life that gets terrorized by terror, not death. Banaras, the dwelling place of ghosts, spirits, the defeated, the undead. How can you scare them? Banaras laughs and prays for those who die and for those who kill. Within twenty-four hours of the bomb blast, Banaras came back to life—back in every bell which echoed, in the Ganga-Jamuna rivers as they flowed, in the surge and flourish of bhaang, in the dawn breaking on every ghat.

'Hey, you know, there was a blast at the station too. It made a three-inch-deep crater!' Jaivardhan said.

'Yes, and bombs were found in a dustbin and at a cinema hall also. The squad defused then,' I said.

'Those are just rumours, man. Idiots cause so much chaos at times like these,' Dada said.

'They were saying in the news that there was a wedding at the temple. It was a cooker that blasted,' I said.

'Man, they make a bomb out of anything these days! How many things can you be wary of?' Jaivardhan said, picking up the newspaper.

* * *

Bhagwandas Hostel. The hostel of future lawyers, judges and magistrates. The hostel that was renovated every year and had thousands of nails hammered into its body so that there was not so much as a crease on its children's clothes. The hostel that built a playing field on its chest so it could protect its children from academic stress. The hostel that burnt with a high-mast lamp all night so its children could have a good night's sleep. This hostel, which cared for its children like a father, was also listening to the discussions, stories and rumours of the bomb blast, and it knew whatever its children told it.

But wait! Maybe I was wrong. Maybe the hostel knew more than these discussions. In one of its rooms, things had been a little strange since the day before the blast. One person had become too calm and quiet. He hadn't eaten anything in the mess for the last two days. He would call for food to his room and keep the empty plate outside. He was constantly changing his SIM. He would make one call, then switch off the phone. He was doing the same thing that night, when Navenduji's surprised voice called out, 'Suraj! Dada! Come out, look, what's happening outside?'

'What's happening, Navenduji?'

'Arre!'

'What are these policemen doing in Bhagwandas?' Dada said, leaving the room quickly.

'Come on now, all of you go back to your rooms now. This is a police operation,' a Provincial Armed Constabulary (PAC) constable told us.

'Police operation?'

'In Bhagwandas?'

'What's going on, man?' I asked.

'Arre, yaar!'

'Who are they dragging down?' Dada asked.

'This is . . . '

'This is . . . '

'It's Roshan.'

'Why him?'

'What has he done?' We were all confused, just like Navenduji.

Roshan had his hands tied behind his back and two police officers were holding him by the neck. They dragged him downstairs and put him into the backseat of the PAC van before heading off—all in just a couple of minutes. We were in shock. All of Bhagwandas was in shock. With questions like why, how, when and what, all students approached Murali Sir. He was standing outside with our dean, but refused to say anything, giving the excuse that he did not know anything because it was a police operation. Slowly, the crowd started dissipating from the warden's room, and seeing that we were no closer to finding out anything, we too returned to our room.

'What has Roshan done?' Navenduji asked.

'You would know better,' I said to Navenduji.

'How would I know better? We haven't even spoken in the past four to five months. He would greet me when he passed by but that was all,' Navenduji said softly.

'There was a police raid at 9 p.m.! Something is wrong, very wrong!' Dada said.

'It's quite late, let's go to sleep now. We'll find out something tomorrow,' Navenduji said, leaving the room.

The next morning, rumours were flying without heads, tails or wings, from one ear to the other. There were as many stories as there were people. Amid these rumours, we also heard that Roshan Chaudhuri's room had been checked in the presence of the warden and then sealed.

It was the third night after the incident. The pressure of our upcoming projects and presentations had prevented us from thinking of anything else. When there was no news in the paper, we assumed Roshan had been arrested in connection to some case in his village. This rumour had been going around and it seemed like the only logical explanation. That night, too, I did not realize anything and fell asleep while talking to Shikha. I woke up to a loud knock on my door.

'Abey, who is it?' I asked.

'Proctor,' a voice echoed from the other side.

It was natural for any mention of the proctor to send shivers down a hosteler's spine. This was B.H.U's own security wing. Being faced with this wing that was full of ex-army officers could give goosebumps to the best of the best. Their job was to maintain peace in such a large university.

The proctor's arrival at this time of the night was a sign that things were not all right. Something seemed out of place.

'Dada, the proctor is here. We don't have a heater in our room, do we?' I whispered.

'No. But it's 3 a.m., what's the problem? Open the door.'

'Yes?' I said, opening the door.

'Are you Anurag and Suraj?' asked the proctor.

'Yes. But what's the matter?'

'You will have to come to the proctor's office.'

'Now? At this hour?'

'Yes. We have told your warden and taken his permission. Come.'

Some people had woken up because of the sound of the proctor's car arriving at night. Everyone was dumbfounded at these incidents taking place in the hostel. I was embarrassed to be sitting in the proctor's car like this, that too when familiar people were looking at us with suspicious eyes. Anyway, we were compelled to sit inside. Jaivardhan had also woken up, but before he could ask us anything, the car had left for the proctor's office.

* * *

'Is your name Suraj?' the proctor asked me as soon as I entered his office.

'Yes, Sir,' I replied.

'Show me your identity card,' he said, holding his hand out.

'Sorry, Sir?' I asked, a bit surprised.

'Don't you understand English? I said, show me your identity card,' the proctor said harshly.

'I lost it, Sir,' I said truthfully.

'Oh? Then you must have reported it in the office?'

'No, Sir,' I said, looking down.

'Great! You must have applied for a new identity card or did you not bother with that either?' the proctor thundered.

'No, Sir,' I replied, still looking down.

'This is the problem with the young generation. Nothing in the world is important to you except enjoyment, fun and games. Do you know that your carelessness, which you call a small matter, could have landed you in big trouble? Your life and career would have been ruined, and your family would have died making trips to the court and back. You're a law student, aren't you? I can fully understand what you are going to teach others after leaving this place. This one act of carelessness could have put you on the most-wanted list,' the proctor said in a single breath. After staring at me for a few seconds, he turned to Dada.

'And you are Anurag, right?'

'Yes, Sir,' Dada replied quickly.

'You used to have a mobile phone, am I right?' the proctor asked indirectly.

'Yes, Sir, that got lost and I filed a report that day itself. I still have a copy of the report,' Dada said, providing information he had not been asked for.

'It seems you have done one responsible thing in your life, that's why you remember it so well. Anyway, be grateful you were responsible. Here, take your phone back,' the proctor said, returning the phone.

Our eyes widened with surprise and joy when we saw the phone.

'You, kindly take care of your identity card,' the proctor seethed at me.

'Sir. Can I ask you something?' Dada said after building up a great deal of courage.

'I know what you want to ask, but go ahead.'

'Sir, what happened?' Dada asked.

'Something bad has happened and something even worse could have happened to the two of you, but destiny has saved you by a hair.'

What the proctor told us after that was nothing less than a bomb blast. We were left dumbfounded. When he finished speaking, I could only ask one question, 'Sir. How can you trust us?'

'No, I don't trust you. I am no one to interfere in this matter. This is a police case. The police detained Roshan in the matter of the bomb blasts. All of this has been recovered after questioning him. I have already told you the scale of trouble you two could have been in if Anurag had not reported his phone. Anyway, dawn will break soon. Go back to your hostel, focus on your work and give that Bajaj Pulsar of yours some rest.' The proctor delivered two blows at once.

'Thanks, Sir,' we said and left his office.

I checked my phone as soon as I came out. There were ten missed calls from Shikha. I hadn't been able to hear them because my phone was on silent. The story had spread like wildfire. I called her.

'Hello, where are you?' She sounded upset.

'I'm okay.' I gave a careless reply.

'What happened? Why did people from the proctor's office take you? Are you all right? I'm very scared.' Shikha was crying.

'It's nothing, don't worry. I'm all right, I'll meet you tomorrow and tell you everything,' I said.

'And what has Roshan done?' Shikha asked.

'Yaar, do I look like I'm in charge of everyone's business, huh?' I shouted, at which Dada gestured at me to keep calm. Shikha's questions were annoying me.

'Okay . . . okay . . . it's all right. Cool down. I am sorry, I'll talk to you later,' Shikha said hurriedly.

'All right, see you tomorrow,' I said dryly.

'And listen . . . I want to say something . . . '

'What is it now, yaar?' I asked irritatedly.

'I love you.'

On another day, at another time, Shikha saying those words would have meant something else. It would have been the most beautiful moment of my life, a moment which I had been waiting for. But somehow, at this moment, I was turned off.

'I love you too. See you tomorrow. Bye, take care,' I said and disconnected the call.

'Wanna go to Assi Ghat?' Dada asked.

'Let's go,' I said, and we started walking towards it.

Saajish: Conspiracy

Assi Ghat. The first ghat when you go northwards. The ghat where the Varuna and Assi rivers meet. The ghat of saints, the ghat of swindlers. The ghat of poets, the ghat of pictures. The smokers' ghat, the drinkers' ghat. My ghat. Dada's ghat. Our ghat.

We had just sat down after coming from the proctor's office when Jaivardhan called from the hostel phone.

'Where are you, dude?' he asked.

'At Assi Ghat.'

'Assi Ghat? The people from the proctor's office left you in Gangaji, huh?'

'We're just sitting here. Why don't you come too?'

'At 4 a.m.? Nobody's getting proper sleep here in the hostel. First that Roshan went, then you two went. Now you're saying you're sitting at Assi Ghat! Is everything all right?'

'Just come, man. Don't act like the CBI,' I snapped and disconnected the call.

There were a few moments of silence. Both of us were stunned, and not in a state to say anything. Assi Ghat was only just beginning to wake up—a beggar was dragging a bowl on the ground, a young girl was insisting we buy a flower garland. Ultimately, I broke the silence.

'I think this is what Dubey was talking about.'

'What?' Dada spoke so softly that I would not have been able to hear him if it wasn't so quiet.

'That something big is going to happen.'

'How would Dubey know?' Dada asked gravely.

'No. man. He definitely exaggerates things, but he doesn't talk nonsense. And, anyway, he had found out from someone connected to the proctor. Now that I think of it, Dubey had also said on the day of the match that Roshan works in some garage at night. Maybe it was for all this,' I said, taking a long breath.

Dada was silent. Actually, he was upset. The thought that he was cheated had saddened him. There were a few more moments of grave silence. We kept watching the Ganga flow without talking to each other. The silence was broken for the second time when Jaivardhan arrived and said, 'What happened, guys? Why are you sitting here all of a sudden? There's no problem, right? I hope everything is all right.'

'There was a problem. There isn't anymore,' I said.

'What do you mean?' asked Jaivardhan.

'You remember the three cookers in Roshan's room?' I said as soon as Jaivardhan sat down.

'Yes, so what? Did the proctor take Roshan away for a single cooker?'

'No, man. Cooker bombs were used in the blast.'

'What do you mean?' Jaivardhan asked, taken aback.

'I mean that Roshan was involved in the bomb blasts. That's why he has been detained.'

'What do you mean? How? Damn it, you mean Roshan Chaudhari!' Jaivardhan was staggered.

'Yes. Roshan Chaudhari. Son of Ishtiyak Chaudhari,' Dada said, stressing on his name.

'Oh my god! Yaar, we didn't know this at all!' Before Jaivardhan could say anything more, I started to repeat what we had found out just a while ago.

'Roshan took admission here so he could orchestrate the blast. Shashank's attempt to call a spirit, my fight at Lanka, the Shivdaspur raid, Dada's mobile being stolen, all of it was part of the plan.'

'Roshan wanted the hostel room from the first day itself. His aim was to plan the blast. That's why he argued so much with the warden. Once he got a place in the hostel, his biggest problem was his roommate. It was essential for him to live alone to carry out these activities. That's why he made up the spirit story. Shashank's behaviour had made it clear to him that he was depressed and had suicidal tendencies. That's why Roshan hatched the spirit plan, and he got help, unintentionally, from Shashank and his suicide attempt. A student with suicidal tendencies is not allowed to stay in a hostel anyway. Plus, Shashank's father came and took him away. That's how Roshan got a single room. Now, I have a feeling that if you matched the handwriting, you would realize that Shashank wasn't the one writing all those creepy things in his room. Shashank must have locked the door from the outside so Roshan wouldn't foil his suicide attempt. This mistake gave Roshan an opportunity—he took the chance, and he wrote those things,' Dada said, scraping the Assi Ghat stairs with a piece of wood.

'Hmm . . . what came next?' Jaivardhan asked.

'That day, when Shashank went to the bathroom to attempt suicide, he locked the door from the outside so Roshan would not try to save him. And when Roshan was waiting for someone to come out of their rooms, we were the only ones, because at 2 p.m. most people head for a nap. We're the only people who eat that late. So, unfortunately, we were the people who got caught up in all this. After that, Roshan started to implicate us,' I said.

'How can you say that?' Jaivardhan asked.

'My fight at Lanka, the Shivdaspur episode, Dada's stolen phone—everything is connected to this,' I said.

'What?' Jaivardhan could not understand.

'Yes. The tasks assigned to Roshan were to provide materials for the blast, to email the media right after it and then arrange for their boys to make a run for it. It wasn't hard to arrange the materials, but the job post the blast was more difficult. First, tickets had to be arranged. These days, they need at least one ID proof for four tickets. That's why Roshan engineered a fake fight at Lanka and those boys stole my ID card. Everyone knew about my friendship with Shikha, so even I thought that was the reason. But the truth is that the fight was just for the ID card, so they could escape easily using tickets bought in my name.'

'Oh my god! This sounds like a detective film! And then?' Jaivardhan was agitated.

'His next task was to send the email after the blast, for which he needed the Internet. That's why he needed an Internet zone which was not password-protected. I think he heard our conversation about the CrPC question paper, which means he too found out that Murali Sir did not have much knowledge about computers. His expert must have also told him that Murali Sir's Wi-Fi was not password-protected. That's why he went and told Murali Sir that Suraj was good at Hindi, so that he would ask me to write the Hindi speech,' I said.

'But yaar! I had gone to the library and told Kamlesh indirectly that that you were good in Hindi. Then how did Roshan tell Murali Sir?' Jaivardhan asked a good question.

'Absolutely. You meant to tell Kamlesh, but Roshan was sitting right behind you. He's the one who told Murali Sir. Roshan knew there was no Internet in the hostel, so to transfer any documents, we would have to use a pen drive or a floppy. Once a pen drive or floppy is plugged into a computer, expert hackers can hack that computer's IP address. That's the reason he told Murali Sir about my Hindi and even lent his pen drive, so we would take the document to Murali Sir's computer. And then he took the pen drive to his expert hacker,' I said, taking a sharp breath.

'So, it was certain that there was going to be a blast and the email would be sent after that. Now, the email was sent from a computer near Bhagwandas Hostel, and they knew that students of the hostel whose names were in the police record would be suspected right away. They hatched the Shivdaspur plan to put our names in the police record.'

'That means . . . ' Jaivardhan was solving crossword puzzles in his head.

'That means that Roshan wanted our names to somehow appear in the police record once, so that the police would arrest us first and foremost. That's why he made up the story, disguised Narhari as a labourer and sent him to us. He wanted us to somehow rescue the girl alone, so our names would be registered in the police record and it would become easier for the police to arrest us after the blast. But he got annoyed when we mentioned the NGO. He realized that this would ensure our safety. That's why he stormed out of our room that day,' I said.

'One more thing. No girl was actually sold there; it was just Roshan's ploy to get our names into the police record. That's why he gave the girl a Bengali name, Rimpa, so I would definitely try to save her. That's also why she did not understand me when I spoke to her in Bengali. She told the police her real name, Jebunnisa. We're so stupid, we didn't even question why a labourer would approach us and nobody else in such a large university!' Dada said.

'He did go! He went to that boy from Birla!' Jaivardhan said.

'Has anyone seen that boy? Has anyone met him? Does he even exist?' asked Dada.

'Oh, damn! Yaar, I didn't even realize this! You mean there was nobody from Birla Hostel there? There was no such boy at all? Damn, this is a whole conspiracy! My god! One man fucking fooled the whole hostel. I mean, that Roshan, we were like puppets in his hands!' Jaivardhan said, downcast

'Absolutely,' Dada said.

'And was Narhari involved in this as well?'

'Who knows? None of the people who were caught are called Narhari. Maybe he gave a false name. It's also possible he was a labourer who was paid to do this,' Dada said.

'But why didn't all this happen? I mean, how did Roshan let you two go?' Jaivardhan asked suddenly.

'Roshan had made all the arrangements, but he needed a phone for communication. That's why he stole Dada's phone. He thought we would look for the phone for a while and then forget about it. Then he would trap us by using the phone before and after the blast. But Dada immediately registered an FIR with the police, and this upset his whole plan. He knew the police surveillance team would be alerted if the phone was used. So, the plan had to be changed. He had to distract the police. When we didn't fall into the trap, he must have laid it for someone else. And the proctor's office probably helped us because they found the identities of those people who were being implicated when the same could not be done with us.'

'Who?' Jaivardhan asked.

'No idea. The proctor didn't tell us that, but it must have been someone careless like us. Actually, Roshan had been on a look out for careless students ever since he joined. He observed our manners, our routine, our carelessness, and he thought us fit for this task. That's why he tried to implicate us,' Dada said.

'And those who actually planted the bombs? Where are they?' Jaivardhan asked.

'Now that's the police's job. I'm sure they'll find out,' I said.

'But how did this massive reveal happen so quickly?' Jaivardhan continued his barrage of questions.

'Even spirits break down under police torture, and it wasn't like Roshan was someone hardcore, he was ideology-driven. He must have weakened when the police beat him. Or maybe he didn't regret anything and confessed the details proudly,' Dada said.

'What luck you were blessed with, guru! Otherwise Roshan had made arrangements for you to serve fourteen years. Forget becoming a lawyer, your life would have gone by in pursuing lawyers. You wouldn't have gone to court to approve bail, but to ask for it!' Jaivardhan laughed.

'Yeah, man! Just been thinking what would have happened if I weren't so lucky,' Dada said.

Gangaji had started to redden. The sun's rays, like every day, had begun to wash her feet. Assi Ghat was also welcoming its boatmen, florists, priests and tea vendors. Sandalwood was being smeared in preparation of the puja. The crows were calling from every direction. We got up to go to the hostel.

It was morning.

Ek Din Achanak: Suddenly, One Day

The bomb blast took place before the last semester. The incident and its possible consequences left a mark on Dada and me for days. The last semester, however, was closing in, so we had no option but to forget about the incident. We were trying to leave it behind us in our last days at Bhagwandas. The meeting of friends and the noting of their phone numbers had begun. We were all going to miss these three years in Bhagwandas Hostel. Some people were going to miss them a little less—the ones who were going to start a career in a law firm or under an advocate-on-record. Some, a little more—the ones who had to start preparing for a career as a judicial or legal officer. The ones who would miss them the most were those who were unable to decide what they wanted to do.

The exam dates were out. It was time for the final presentations. Dada and Jaivardhan were in a different group and their presentations were over. That day was my group's presentation. It was going to be a while before my turn came to present. Dada had brought his father's case files to the hostel and started to look at them. He often joked that he wanted to run his father's law firm, and in any case, his father was a well-known lawyer in Mughalsarai and Banaras. Jaivardhan had also been confirmed by the law firm Mehra and Mehra. He had to join soon after the exams got over. I could only see a dark future before me. I was confused between advocacy, a master's degree and a job. I was sitting amid these questions in the classroom, waiting for my presentation, when my phone started vibrating. It was a message from Shikha, 'Meet me . . . now.'

'I can't. Presentation is going on,' I replied.

'Forget about the presentation . . . and come . . . fast,' she replied immediately.

I couldn't quite digest that Shikha was saying no to the presentation. She could do anything, but never say no to studies. What had happened that she was asking me to come immediately and that too leaving the presentation behind? What if her parents wanted to meet me? Maybe they had come and Shikha had told them about me? But Shikha wouldn't tell her family without asking me. Then why had she called me out of the blue? What if she was in trouble?

'Where?' I asked quickly.

'Pizzeria,' her answer came at once.

My god! Must be a treat. But in the afternoon? I thought and texted again. 'Are you serious?'

'I am damn serious, my love. Come fast and no more texting.'

Now I wasn't left with an option. If Shikha had said it was serious, then it must be. I started to get up with the presentation paper in my hands. As soon as I stood up, Murali Sir announced, 'By the way, all of you must be aware that today is the last day of presentations.'

I realized this was directed at me, but I really didn't have a choice. I said, 'Sir, can I be excused for a minute?'

'Can't you wait for some time?'

'Sir, I can wait but nature can't,' I replied directly, and the class burst into laughter.

'You may go. But please make sure to return before 2 p.m. This is the last day.' Murali Sir knew every inch of me.

'Sure, sir,' I said and left the class. On the way, I kept thinking what day it was. Birthday? No, that was 10 July. I hadn't even proposed on this date! Rose Day, Valentine's Day, there was nothing! Then what was the occasion? Why was she calling me to the Pizzeria? I carried the confusion to the Pizzeria.

I was stunned the moment I entered. Dada and Jaivardhan were also there with Shikha. This was unusual because Shikha had never spoken to my friends in the last three years. Neither Dada nor Jaivardhan had ever tried to talk to her. I couldn't understand anything anyway, and the meaningful smiles on their faces were making me even more worried. In any case, I thought it would be better if I didn't look too worried. I pulled up an empty chair and said, 'What's up, guru? There's a whole party gathered here, what happened?'

'You just order, man. Don't ask questions,' Dada said.

'Huh? Even people crashing a wedding find out who's getting married! Will someone tell me what this party is for, and who's giving it?'

'You're giving it,' Shikha smiled. This smile and the strange feeling around it confused me more. I was a bit annoyed. 'If you had to play a prank like this, you should have at least let me make my presentation! I left the presentation midway.'

'Maybe you don't need it.' Shikha smiled her meaningful smile once more.

'Why?' I asked, surprised.

'Because . . .

You . . .

Have . . .

Been . . .

Selected . . .

For . . .

Section Officer!!!' Shikha shouted every word and Dada and Jaivardhan also started to hoot with her.

I could not understand anything. How were the results for an interview I took over a year ago being announced now? And even if they were, had I really been selected?

'Another prank, am I right?' I refused to believe it.

'No, my friend! You don't play the fool with life. The result came just today. Shikha has been checking the SSC website almost every day. When the result was declared, Shikha called me first and said we'll tell you after it gets confirmed. This plan was made after your father's name was confirmed with your admit card. See it for yourself,' Dada said, handing me the printout.

I kept admiring my name on the printout. I ran my fingers over it multiple times. When you have given up all hope for something and it comes to you, it becomes even more difficult to believe it. For a man, tears are his greatest treasure. He does not spend them needlessly. Maybe my tears had been waiting for this moment all this while, so they flowed out. These eyes had seen so many rejections, so many insults and so many failures that it was tough for them to believe this. Shikha was standing with her hands on mine and her face on my shoulder, while my friends were busy cutting the pizza into slices.

'Dada, have you brought the bike?' I asked suddenly.

'Yes, why?'

'Give me the keys,' I said.

'But Shikha is right here, where will you go now?' Dada said, throwing me the keys.

'Shikha! Please don't mind, can I say something?' I asked her.

'Say!' Shikha said, taken aback.

'I'll just make my presentation and be back. You guys enjoy your pizza until then.'

'Go on,' Shikha laughed.

'There you go! Absolutely. Everyone thinks of the Ramcharitmanas in their old age. He has, too, in his sixth semester!' Everyone laughed out loud when Jaivardhan said this.

I left for the faculty, still laughing. On the way out, I vaguely heard what Jaivardhan was asking Shikha: 'So, when are you two getting married?'

Author's Note

Every book has its own journey, and in this, the translation of the book is an important milestone. The story of *Banaras Talkies* and my knowledge of the language was enough for it to be written in Hindi. But I did wish for it to be translated into other languages, particularly English. Since *Banaras Talkies* was my very first book, this desire was more.

I could not have imagined the kind of acclaim that I have received for *Banaras Talkies* over the years. Its appreciation in literary magazines, newspapers, forums and among people is such that even today, I receive the maximum number of questions and mails regarding this book. My name, and that of my books, in the country and abroad, is because of *Banaras Talkies*.

Readers have been waiting for it to be adapted into a film or a web series. And there's been a demand for the book to be translated into English for a long time—now that is a reality.

If I say that I have woven the entire world of *Banaras Talkies* in my imagination, that would be wrong. Even if a story is fictional, the character picks up the tone from the surroundings. So *Banaras Talkies* is as fictional as you think and as factual as you can understand. That's why my request is to read it as fiction, although I know that your first question after reading it will be: 'Sir, is this story real?'

I am thankful to my editor, Elizabeth Kuruvilla, my literary, agent Kanishka Gupta, the translator, Himadri Agarwal, as well as Penguin Random House India, for coming out with this edition of the book.

Happy reading!

Translator's Note

Of all the places one can choose to translate a campus novel in, nothing gets better than a campus itself. It means that you can attend classes with the characters, catch meals in the mess with them; it means that you can find your characters lurking in hostels and lawns and laundry rooms, watch them discussing professors and assignments and romance and cricket and all the other things that make college students, college students. The first, and one of the best, pieces of advice I got as I translated *Banaras Talkies* was to listen— to listen to the crowds in the corridors between classes, to the throngs of people entering the mess at mealtimes. I had to keep my ears pricked so I could catch snippets of conversation—Dada's quiet maturity in a fourth-year's discussion with a first-year student, a Film Society member who referenced movies not unlike Navenduji, an immature anger that was unmistakably Jaivardhan's. It is the mastery of Satya Vyas' character creation that I can find students from Banaras Hindu University even in a swanky private college nearly a thousand miles away from where the novel was set.

This does not mean that *Banaras Talkies* is not local. It is, in fact, refreshingly, unapologetically so. Vyas does not hold back, whether it is with his characters, with the setting, and, most strikingly, with language. This book has no pretensions about itself—it is loud and it is hilarious. Hindi, English and Bhojpuri do not clash; they mix and do not merge. As a translator, this was a bit nerve-wracking. How much Bhojpuri would I keep? How much Hindi? How would I indicate which language it was from? *Banaras Talkies* is extraordinarily rich in language, so would I be doing it an injustice by bringing it all into English?

Put that way, it seemed rather bleak. But to me, this novel has a potential that I did not feel deserved to be restricted to Hindi readers. Moreover, if translations were to be abandoned just because translating is a risky endeavour, we would never have read many great books. At the start, I believed that what I was attempting to do was almost a failed pursuit, but an exciting one. While my sense of adventure got me to start typing, it didn't change the fact that I was travelling from three languages to one, a journey that was meaningful, profound and incredibly enjoyable, but never easy.

There were several decisions to be made, some trivial (is it Banaras, Benares, or Benaras?) and some more hefty. The major challenge, considering the multilingual nature of my original, was how to distinguish them in my translation, how to ensure that my English readers felt the comfort, grit and sheer punch in Satya Vyas' language. Translation is, at one level, about recreating a reading experience. If I laughed at the characters' jokes, rooted for them when they were in trouble and found myself standing next to them and having a conversation, my hope is for English readers to inhabit those spaces and be a part of that dialogue. If I had gone blindly, translating word by word, metaphor by metaphor, I would had lost the very dynamism that made *Banaras Talkies* so exciting. The book is a linguistic adventure, and I could not, in good faith, take that away from my translation.

I chose retention—to retain words and phrases from the original, particularly ones that were 'un-translatable', or hard to find equivalents for. What I like about this is its humility. When you choose to retain parts of the original, you admit to the insufficiencies of language and to your own insufficiency as a translator. Such words are accused of being alienating to readers, but that is also the beauty of reading. There is something special about being able to read and enjoy a text without understanding every word of it.

The book, ultimately, is in English, so I had to find ways to bring to life, in English, the strains of laughter, of culture and of Bollywood, that live as a language underneath the story Satya Vyas is telling. Take, for instance, the ragging scene, when the seniors make quip after quip on Dubeyji's father. In the original, Dubeyji's father's name is Shridhar Dubey, and the joke is around the word 'dhar', which literally means 'to hold'. It is a sexual reference, but not the same as the one in my translation and nowhere near as explicit. I did have to change the father's name and raise the scale of the joke a little, but I would choose those changes over compromising on the emotion or the humour of the text. From Shilpa Shetty's letter and the creepy poem in Roshan's room to Jaivardhan's idioms and his particularly colourful expletives, I have been quite experimental with regard to *Banaras Talkies*. The letter, in fact, is the part I translated at the very end—Bieber and Maroon 5 are hardly the equivalent of retro Bollywood, but a shared experience of music existed in the background of that letter, and since I could not summon Bollywood, another musical community became my refuge in translating it.

Adrenaline is starkly underrated when it comes to translation. There is sheer excitement in having a text on one side of your laptop and a blank document on the other, of going down page by page of the text and your translation alike and discovering, quite suddenly, that you have reached the end. Unlike writing, where your mind needs to keep searching for content, translation is a readymade, action-packed adventure. Once the initial few pages are up, it becomes a groove, a fun-filled and rather calming experience, something of the nature of knitting or gardening. It is easy to feel alone when one reads or writes, and even though translation takes place in isolation, there is the constant presence of an author and a text which reminds the translator that she is not doing this by herself. In fact, this has the potential to be rather intimidating—the joy of translation comes with both accountability and responsibility.

Translation, like most art, is eternally incomplete, and we must learn to make peace with it. Self-doubt is easy to encounter, and while it fuels excellence, it also begins to pull one back after a point. I know that my work on *Banaras Talkies* is miles away from perfect and, even then, I would not change a thing. It is ridden with mistakes and can be questioned at nearly every sentence, but that (along with my own insufficiency) is the nature of the discipline and the beauty of the text. There has been a lot of learning, a lot of laughing and a little bit of falling in love, and I am grateful for every second.

Here, I must clarify that I cannot take credit for this translation. It belongs, first and foremost, to Satya Vyas, for his masterpiece. To the Ashoka Centre for Translation and Arunava Sinha. To Mumma, Papa, Didi, Jiju, Ekta Di, Bhaiya and Bhabhi. To Astha, Aditiya, Manas, Mukesh, Pragya, Preksha, Vartika and Uday. To Ajita Sircar, Ruma Sen, Damayanti Mukherjee, and Menoka Yadav. To the lovely Penguin Random House team. To every person involved in its writing and translation, and to every reader who is kind enough to read it.